# DRACULA
## BEYOND STOKER

### Issue 2

DBS Press

*Dracula Beyond Stoker*
Issue 2

Tucker Christine
editor

Edward G. Pettit
consulting editor

Published by DBS Press
ISBN - 979-8-9867340-4-0 (Paperback)
ISBN - 979-8-9867340-5-7 (e-book)
May, 2023

www.dbspress.com
www.draculabeyondstoker.com

# Contents

29 April

My Dear Loyal Reader,

Welcome to Dracula Beyond Stoker, Issue 2. The Renfield Issue.

Renfield is arguably the most fascinating character in Stoker's novel, and one of the most intriguing in all of literature. He's a remarkable feat for a writer in that he has next to no backstory, what little backstory we do get is unreliable and unverifiable, and his motivations and loyalties waver. It can take multiple readings to understand what bearing his presence has on the narrative, yet he can easily and instantly become many readers' favorite character.

The lack of detail, yet complexity of character makes him ideal for this project, as he's ripe for interpretation. In the following pages we are delighted to present ten brand new Renfield tales featuring unique takes on Dr. Seward's pet lunatic. Some present a Renfield you will recognize instantly, some will surprise and astound you. You may even find yourself a little unsettled at times. But that's why we read horror, right?

Toothpickings returns with an essay exploring how little we actually know about the Flyman and his origins. We've unearthed "Renfield's Wife" — a classic reprint from Damon Cavalchini, and we conclude with a dark and provocative poem by Elizabeth McClellan.

We hope you enjoy the madness we've assembled for you.

The blood is the life,

Tucker

# FRESH BLOOD

# The Matter of Vivacity

## By Kai Holmwood

Renfield paced laps around his small room, his steps falling into the familiar pattern: four down the room, three across, four back up the room, three across. He had learned to mediate the length of each step to perfectly fit the space. All in all, it was not entirely bad. He had managed to keep his spirits up with the thought that it could not possibly be long before the mistake was recognized and he was released. He swatted at the maddening fly that insisted on buzzing past him — the only thing, other than the minor issue of his confinement, that could dampen his spirits.

Perhaps writing a letter would help to prove his case. He sat at the small desk, picked up the half-century-outdated feather quill they insisted on making him use rather than a sharp steel-tipped pen for some unfathomable reason, dipped it into the watered-down ink — he was accustomed to far better, given his station and occupation, but he would manage — and began to write.

*15 May. —*

*Dear Dr. Seward, my esteemed sir,*

*I have heard the attendant report to you that, at certain periods, I "lack vivacity." Perhaps this is the reason you generously insist upon extending my stay here. May I remind you, sir, that the poet William Blake wrote the following lines:*

*A robin red breast in a cage*

*Puts all Heaven in a rage*

*Thus in a humble effort to ease the raging burdens of Heaven by securing my release from this cage, I present to you the following case (though I note the exceptional difficulty of crafting an organized argument as a fly buzzes around my head, and protest the unfairness of being kept in such conditions):*

*"Vivacious" comes from the Latin vivere, "to live." It might best be defined as meaning "full of life."*

*Surely you will concede that there can be no creature that is both dead and alive simultaneously, sir. One is either a corpse or one is alive.*

*Have you ever, I inquire, received a letter from a corpse, or heard evidence of a corpse writing a letter? If not, sir, I say you have no choice but to release me immediately. The logic is inarguable:*

*(1.) You are reading this letter, therefore/a fortiori:*

*(2.) The man who wrote this letter (by whom I mean myself, sir) is not a corpse, a fortiori:*

*(3.) I am alive, a fortiori:*

*(4.) I am full of life, id est "vivacious," and thus cannot by definition "lack vivacity." Quod erat demonstrandum; the argument is thus proven, along with my case.*

Renfield set down the quill carefully so that the tip would not drip its last drop of ink upon the desk. It mattered little; the surface was already blotted and stained, with some of the marks so dark and fresh that they might have been made yesterday. Except that *he* had been in this room for several weeks, and thus the marks must have been older than they looked.

He leaned back in his simple chair, reaching within his mind for the next step of his argument. It had all been so easy decades before, in his law school days, but now it felt as if the sharp memory were hovering about the edge of his mind, with the center clouded and blurred. A condition of age, no doubt, though at fifty-nine years old, he was still vital. *Vivacious*, if he did say so himself.

Nor were all of his memories obscured by that cloud. More recent ones, as of his library, were still sharp. He walked the remembered room, letting his mind's eye explore one shelf after another in search of something to support his argument. He ignored the law books; he knew everything within. His imagination lighted on one specific volume, and he imagined pulling it from the shelf. It felt almost real in his hand. This would do.

Renfield was surprised to find himself on his feet by the door of his confinement. As he had walked in his mind, so, too, must he have unconsciously walked through this small room. He returned to the desk and the letter.

*The attendant must be both wrong and frightfully unobservant. He evidently cannot distinguish a living man from a corpse. How could he be qualified to assess my condition if he cannot tell if I am alive or dead?*

*Have you ever read the decades-old Irish tale of the vampire Carmilla, sir? I shall loan you the copy from my library upon my release. Perhaps the attendant has read that ghastly tale of the vampire woman who, neither dead nor alive, escaped her tomb to feed upon the blood of young women. Perhaps he has mistaken fiction for truth. Again, sir, I wish to point out his unreliability and unsuitability for the task of assessing whether my condition is suitable for release.*

That would do, Renfield thought. Writing about *Carmilla* would force Dr. Seward to confront the absurdity of the attendant's implications. No one could believe such a creature would truly exist, and thus, his case was proven. Quod erat demonstrandum.

But what if someone like Carmilla *could* exist? Imagine how vivacious — *vivacious!* — she would be. He had, despite his better judgment, been drawn to that particular woman ever since he had read the book, oh, how many years ago was it? Time was a blur. It didn't matter.

Something about her reminded him of a sleek, lithe, predatory cat.

When he had been a boy, the family had had a cat.

He had seen the devilish creature once with half of a sparrow clasped between its teeth, feathers splayed about and drifting away in the faintest puff of breeze. The feline's eyes were wide and dark, and its tail swished with pride and defiance, as if it were warning him not to even dare steal its precious, life-giving supper.

That was the image he had always seen in his mind's eye when he read of Carmilla.

*Have you ever peered into a cat's eyes just after it has caught and eaten its feathered supper, still pulsing with vitality as it goes down the feline's gullet? If you have, sir, you will understand the link I have explained to you between vivacity and life.*

*Nothing is so vivacious as a cat who has just eaten a bird, or a mouse.*

*Nothing is so full of life.*

*Quod erat demonstrandum I do not belong in this confinement, sir.*

But what of the cat?

He fought to remember. He had been so young.

He had lured the cat to his room with promises of food. That much, at least, he remembered.

His father had never liked him — the cat. He had died young — the father, not the cat — younger than he, Renfield, was now. He had jumped out the window — the cat, not the father — to the ground far below and run into the darkness while he, Renfield, waited.

He had disappeared. He had come back with a feather in his mouth. He had never come back. He had hunted. He had waited and watched. He had — he hadn't — which he?

Renfield couldn't remember quite what he had been thinking. He found himself sucking the tip of his feather quill as he mused. In a moment of sudden awareness, he laughed at the thought of himself like the childhood cat, sitting there with a feather in his mouth. It tasted rather unpleasant, but that was to be expected given that it was likely from a bird of prey; making a quill from a sparrow's or pigeon's feather would be absurd. It must, he thought, be from a falcon.

Perhaps that was the reason humans always ate prey instead of predators; perhaps animals who eat animals all taste unpleasant.

It was proper manners to include some small talk and pleasantries in a letter, even when one was writing for a specific purpose. Renfield set to work.


*Is it not interesting that so few species eat carnivores? Cats are one of the few creatures that do not discriminate, eating smaller animals regardless of diet. I believe a cat would eat a falcon as gladly as a sparrow or a pigeon.*


What else could he write? There was so little to tell here. All he had were his thoughts. They did not even permit him books. What was he meant to include in a letter? How could they expect him to include anything? How dare they expect him to make polite pleasantries? How dare they keep him here — *him*, the esteemed R. M. Renfield, solicitor?

He gritted his teeth, forcing air through them slowly. He must calm himself if he wished to get out. The damn godforsaken attendant had always spoken highly of his pleasantness and sanguine temperament, and no doubt Dr. Seward would take that into account.

And yet the question stood: what else might he write about in this letter to demonstrate his sanity, his pleasantness, his manners, his propriety? All he had here were his thoughts and his dreams.

He had dreamed of everlasting life. Of soaring through the night sky, eternal, ageless, his blood throbbing with vitality. Vivacity. But how to describe that in a letter? Besides, dreams were not fit for sharing; only the mannerless and the mad insisted on sharing their dreams.

Only the mad. That, at least, would help him. Quod erat demonstrandum.

*They say the mark of a madman is that he speaks of his dreams as if they were real. I will tell you nothing of my dreams, sir, and thus prove my sanity and further quod my demonstrandum.*

His head was starting to ache. The fly would *not* leave him alone.

He had heard that flies lived for only a day. How long had this one been circling him? An hour? A week? A lifetime? His lifetime or the fly's?

He stood at the window, staring at the ground far below. Then he glanced across his room to the writing desk. A quill sat there dripping onto the stained surface. He had been writing — but why?

That damned fly.

What was it Blake had written?

"The clever cat that eats the fly

Shall live long past his day to die"

How was it still so unexhausted, so full of life?
*Vivacious.*
Fortiori demonstrandum.
He returned to the writing desk.

*I have told you that "vivacious" comes from the Latin vivere, that it means "full of life." Thus I tell you now: little is more vivacious, more literally FULL of LIFE, sir, than a cat who has eaten a mouse who has eaten a spider &c. &c.*
*Vivacious, I tell you. Quod fortiori.*

He dropped the quill and pressed his hands over his ears, trying to block out the maddening buzz. Rage was swelling through him. He would kill the damnable fly. Kill it.

As he lifted his hand to smite the creature, which had alighted on the wall beside where he lay, the golden evening sunlight caught on its wings, sending them into rainbows of beauty. He let his hand fall to the floor. Even the smallest of animals, he reminded himself, contained the most precious gift of all: the gift of life. Vitality. Vivacity.

That reminded him of the letter he had been writing a day or two before. He might as well finish it. He pushed himself from the floor to his feet and walked to the desk, sat down, and lost himself in thoughts of the rainbow worlds in a fly's wings.

*"To see a world in a grain of sand*
*and Heaven in the wings of a fly."*
*Blake wrote those lines, sir. The smallest part of a whole contains all. To hold eternity in an hour. Thus quod erat if you answer one riddle, sir, you will understand all the world. A demonstrandum. I present you your riddle.*
*How many lives contained in one? Three mice in a cat. What was in the mouse?*
*"A cat all fill'd with doves & pigeons*

*Shudders Hell thr' all its regions"*

He had never felt that he understood Blake — not until now. The cat all filled with falcons. The falcons all filled with mice. The mice all filled with spiders. Lives within lives within lives.

The world went silent and still as it all came together.

He had solved it all. He knew the secret that tied together the clues they had left behind for him: lithe Carmilla, clever Blake, even the childhood cat who had stood proud over a half-eaten bird, gazing at the boy who would someday grow into a man who would understand all of the hints that they had all left just for him.

He began humming happily, cheered beyond measure by the secret that swelled within him. He was special. He was chosen. He alone would carry the knowledge forward. No one else could understand. But just as they had all left clues for him, he must leave clues for the next recipient of the sacred secret of everlasting life and immortality. Vivacity.

Mr. Seward had always been good to him. He would leave his hint for Mr. Seward.

*Have you heard it said that cats have nine lives? Perhaps there is some correlation between their diet and their longevity & resilience. The thought is a gift for you to consider, sir, and a token of my goodwill. It contains all of the sacred mysteries.*

Why was he staring out through his door's small window to the hallway? There was naught for him there. His home, the clean home that he half-remembered from years or days or a lifetime ago, was precisely that: clean.

Had he ever seen a fly there? Or a mouse? Or a spider?

He couldn't remember. It didn't matter.

The fly buzzed around his head again, offering its divine sacrifice in service of Life. He opened his mouth to receive the sacrament.

As if to erase any last doubt in Renfield's mind, the moment he took the first fly, another flew in through his window, its wings in the sacred, blessed morning sunlight carrying all the rainbows of Heaven. Quod erat demonstrandum. He was precisely where he was meant to be.

*I understand, of course, your duty to protect the public &c. &c. I assure you, sir, that I am no threat to any human.*

*Sir, I beseech you to pay no heed to my earlier complaints about the unsanitary nature of my chamber and the resulting flies. I shall manage them myself. Someday I shall demonstrate to you that my vivacity exceeds any former limits. Until then, I am pleased to stay here at your discretion. Now I can wait.*

*Yours very respectfully, &c. &c.,*

*R. M. Renfield, solicitor*

"What an absolutely fascinating fellow."

"Might I inquire as to what the letter says, sir?" the attendant asked. "Is he complaining yet again about the flies?"

Dr. Seward folded the letter along its original creases and tucked it away into an inner pocket. "He begins by making a legal argument to prove that he is alive, as if that were in question. The initial argument itself is — more cohesive than one might expect. It is difficult to make out the middle parts of the letter. The ink is terribly smudged and blotted. He seems to be rather egregiously misquoting William Blake and writing about cats, flies, and a riddle that I can't quite make out."

"Is he still attempting to persuade you that he should be set loose upon the city?"

Dr. Seward shook his head. "In the beginning of the letter, he was indeed. In the middle, there is no way of knowing what he desires. By the end, he has returned to his familiar sanguine temperament. He writes clearly, in a steady hand, of his willingness to stay here as long as necessary, and to deal with the flies himself."

**Kai Holmwood** has been a freelance nonfiction writer for over a decade. She recently completed a Master of Writing degree at the University of Canterbury. She and her husband split their time between near-antipodal homes in New Zealand and Portugal.

# Nurse Renfield
## By Laura Keating

When my brother came home, four new locks were bought for our house. One for the door to the attic stairs, two for the upper door to the attic itself, and one for the small round window at the corner of the roof, in the attic. The doctor who was brought in (after the locks) said he'd seen similar cases, but nothing quite like this.

"It's a disease, all right." He hummed as he snapped his large black bag shut. My parents had paid him well for this midnight trip.

"Then we'll have your prescription," said my father. He was a small, no-nonsense man. He had thought of the locks; he disapproved of the doctor. His sister, who lived with us, had made that call. After her cat went missing, before the locks.

"Disease of the mind," said the doctor. "Saw the look all the time after the War."

"My son hasn't been to war," said my mother. She had lost her brother in Ypres, but she did not say so; it was not an uncommon story.

"White foods, cold baths," the doctor went on, swinging on his coat and tugging it closed. He glanced upwards as the sounds began again. "Rest, above all else."

No one noticed me behind the banister. No one noticed me in the best of times. *He* had been their laughing child. *I* was a spider on the beams.

We told our relatives it was exhaustion; his colleagues and our neighbors that it was something caught while abroad. To his old school companions we said nothing — but he was already as forgotten to them as their old raccoon coats and ukuleles. My brother is not a bad man, but he has always had bad taste in friends.

During the day, my mother and father received gifts: preserves and small knit items from the old ladies of the village. Should any of the old dears see it upon themselves to stay for a visit, the radio was kept loud. I served the coffee. I like to be helpful. My mother, not helpful, did not engage in their conversation but sighed at her shoes while uncomfortable looks were exchanged over cups soon clicked back into saucers. Our guests never stayed long and with the door shut and locked behind them, our home would fall once more to its imperfect quiet. Silence would have been terrible, and it would have been better.

During the night, there was nothing to hide the steady, heaving laughter.

Before the locks, there were nightly noises in the hall. A creeping gait, scratching on the doors — I barely noticed. I sleep well. But one night, I spied the top of a head at the foot of my bed. I did not scream (my aunt would have screamed). I waited until two round, white eyes stared back, and he knew I could see him. I could smell the blood on him. The corners of his mouth came up in a black grin, and then he sunk to the floor, sliding under the bed like a dry hand in a stiff glove. I laid still in the middle of my bed while underneath he stayed until the morning when my father pulled him out, shouting and thumping his shoulders with a shoe, my brother cringing like a bad dog as my aunt prayed loudly, palms open and eyes rolled back, in the hallway.

My aunt refused to go near the attic stairs, my mother wept at the thought, and my father would never be so unmanned as to carry a tray. So, it fell to me to bring up the food. I did not mind the attic — although the light was very bad, and I had to put on my glasses. I do not like my glasses, but this is my only vanity.

My brother kept his new room well. He finished all the flies on the windowsill and the rows of dried mice beside the bed were kept very tidy. I have learned not to question the medicine if the effects are satisfactory. When I was able, I brought him other treatments. He was always a bit better after a dose and we could talk. We had never spoken much before, our age difference and genders keeping our worlds apart. He was beginning secondary school when I was born. I was completing my final year at the same school when that ship of rotting nightmares returned him to Whitby. In the past, he'd had friends and he had given me no notice. Now, he depended on my companionship. Only I could provide such sanity. I was, and remain, immensely proud of my work.

P ity is a property of entropy; it becomes diffuse and disordered in time. Calls on the house became less frequent. The hampers of food and little woolens dwindled and then stopped altogether. Neighbors and cousins ceased their enquiries and began to observe my parents with impatience: When could the real mourning begin? There were attempts at discussion about me and my future, but all these conversations still came back to my brother. What was to be done if I were gone?

"I won't be a maid to a madman," my aunt told my father loudly over dinner. We had grown used to the laughter from above — as relentless as the howling of the neighbor's dog — and it stole the taste from our plates. Our food had become dull. "She graduates soon, what then?"

I paid no attention to my aunt's talk. I had no intention of going anywhere. After another tasteless dinner and helping my mother clean up, I asked if I could go for a walk. My father allowed it even though it had gotten dark. They knew the night was always better after I went for a walk.

My parents in their sitting room did not look up when I returned. My father held his paper very still and my mother sewed in minute detail. My aunt, in her room, watched me from her cracked door. She thought I didn't know, but I notice every small thing. I brought a special tray up the attic stairs and for a time there was peace. All was silence outside. The neighbor's dog never barked again.

Our house became a point of speculation. A cold hand on the neck of the village. My aunt moved out and I was glad, but too soon. She had never been a smart woman, a miserable spinster prone to conversation. Whispers spread. Then talk. Who else had lost a chicken, a dog, a cat? Who else had children wake crying of a shadow outside their window? Old stories were shared at the pub, new tales told after church. Had anyone heard of the things that moved on the wings of a bat? Our neighbors were as prone to conversation as my aunt. More urgent enquiries were made about my brother. Could he truly take no callers? Just where had he been? The old ladies of the village delivered prayers in our front garden and my father chased them off. I had to step over the crucifixes and small mirrors laid on the front path to go on my nightly walks. One morning, we woke to find a chain of garlic hung from a nail on the front door. I used it that evening in preparing dinner.

We became reckless. My parents grew fond of the renewed peace, and we forgot the radio. That is why it was not turned on the day my brother's employer, Mr. Johnathan Harker, came to call. His glum wife waited in their new automobile as we welcomed Mr. Harker inside. Standing in our parlor, he explained that some papers requiring the signature of the new tenant of Carfax Hall had gone missing following my brother's trip and he wished to review a file. When the heaving laughter began, the radio was off, and the young solicitor looked sharply up. My parents drew into themselves as the laughter stopped and Mr. Harker delicately enquired over Robert's health. He left soon after.

Dr. Seward's men arrived the next day. My brother was to be taken to the sanitarium in the city. My mother cried; her relief was unmistakable. My father stayed in the sitting room and read his paper, deaf to the yelling and crashes of furniture overhead. Only I was of any help, coaxing my brother from his preferred corner, speaking in the appropriate, soothing tones, and just once required to lie: Yes, darling, of course they'll have your special medicine. The doctor took notice of my skilful management and expressed his gratitude.

"Have you ever considered a career psychiatric care?"

I confessed I had not.

"There are many poor souls that would benefit from such kind treatment."

Would they?

He granted me a smile and left with his pack of orderlies. I quietly watched as my brother was taken away and then I went for a long walk. When I returned, so too had the old dears and the admiration of the village. They gathered about my parents like the wings of a great, protective animal. I went upstairs and packed my bags.

D eath is a common affair at any hospital. My presence eased many a passing — even in the most difficult patients. The staff were thankful for my dutifulness. It was so good to be appreciated. But my primary concern remained one of blood. My brother was of particular interest to Dr. Seward, perhaps owing to the peculiar and gruesome circumstances of his onset madness.

Everyone still remembered the ship.

With no locks on his door, my brother was allowed to wander the hallways alone, to socialize. I disagreed with this treatment, but I was not one to be unhelpful. When he did well, I would turn my attention to more ailing patients, sometimes for a week or sometimes more. What did he need me, and his special medicine, for? In time, my care was certain to be required again.

A suspicious orderly, a mocking whip of a man, began to watch me as I filled charts, trays, and cared for my patients. He disliked my brother and was critical of my talent. I would never complain; I am not the first woman to suffer the jealousy of lesser men. However, it became such that I could not care for my patients as I liked and it was necessary to convalesce after work, to take long walks once more.

Walking is very enjoyable in the city. Hardly anyone knows anyone. But I began to know my way and could get around easily. There are some who would say it is dangerous for a woman to walk alone at night, but that is only because they fear being watched. I am the one who watches. The face at the window, the white hand in the moonlight, the soft footsteps in the dark. One thing I learned at the sanitarium: size is of no matter when you are properly prepared. I am never without my instruments. One never knows when an incident might arise.

Visitors were not uncommon to the sanitarium. Family, occasionally; curious students, more often. The halls provide an unusual diversion. But most often of all, doctors and scholars would tour the facility to see what modern patient care in a good, clean, well-lit place produced. Doctor Seward was a learned man and attracted a circle of the same. Most were gracious and polite and would remark on my loyalty to my brother. But a madman came to our hospital one morning, and the irony was not the least bit funny.

The Madman: a professor, an Englishman of Dutch heritage. He was a stooped, hoary thing, aged beyond his years by his unkindly scowl and bad limp. A prying, bitter, self-aggrandizing man, he took a personal interest in my brother's case — owing chiefly to my brother's condition beginning after his trip to a former Hungarian province. Many young men in the professor's time (the professor included) had gone deep into the continent and returned with parts of themselves missing, some deeper and more essential than others. The professor was curious as to whether my brother's affliction was not of the mind but some infection of the blood. He took samples of my brother's blood. The havoc it caused. Five-point restraints were required for the remainder of the day and night. The doctor and professor had long gone to their brandy and cigars while I stayed long after my shift. The shadows stretched from corners, crept from under the bed, and propagated about the room. The night grew deep, hard cut with white lines of moonlight from the high window. By this critical light, I watched his jaw unclench, his eyes soften and clear, staring first at the ceiling and then, slowly, over at me.

"I don't think I'm getting better," he said.

The next day they took away his spiders.

My walks became more frequent, but less comforting. With the Madman in the halls, I remained in a state of agitation. In such a state, I encountered the tenant of Carfax Hall. By the theatre's golden light, a small group of women with very unhappy escorts buzzed around the tenant like flies on sticky blood. But no escort was quite so unhappy as Mr. Harker. I recognized him and his dreary wife, but she was not so dreary now. Her face had become animated, perhaps lovely, under the penetrating gaze of the remarkable man peering down at her. Tall, elegant, dark, and with the most knowing eyes, together they entered the gilded doors of the playhouse, and as he looked back into the dark street, we crossed glances. In that instant, I was seen to the raw bone. I felt exposed as I never had been, and pulsing with a feeling I mistook for fear I fled from the cutting light of his eyes, running back into the shadow and fog.

The flower girl, the result of my panic, was an accident.

My patient was becoming less cooperative. "I don't think I want that," he told me one day. From the way he was wringing his hands, I knew this to be untrue.

"I could bring you a mouse. A lovely, fat mouse."

He looked away and tried to change the subject, began to speak of a conversation he had overheard, a wild accusation leveled against the tenant of Carfax Hall by the professor, all based, apparently, on a mistaken glimpse in a mirror.

"Perhaps he should be in here, not me, eh?" I waited until his tense, heaving laughter had subsided. "You're angry? Please, don't be angry." But I left all the same. It is not good to linger in the place of the truth.

During the day, I kept to my work and saw to my brother's care, even as he pulled away, even as the mad professor took up more of his time and confidence. It saddened me, this professional estrangement, but I was kept very busy: There was a sudden rush of death at the hospital.

Instincts grow like teeth; buried deep, rising, and finally superseded by something stronger. Mine were sharp. One night, in place of my walk, I decided to check on my brother. He was not in his room. I grew uneasy. I followed my uneasiness down the bone-white corridors towards Dr. Seward's adjoining residence. There were voices echoing softly; distorted, like drips down a deep drain. They became clearer as I drew nearer.

"It has happened again." My brother's voice. "Send me away."

Low, learned murmuring joined in discussion. My shoes slipped easily from my stockinged heels, and I continued down the hallway as silent as a fog.

The large oak door to the doctor's residence was open to the corridor. I stood back from the opening, a shadow amongst the shadows. Inside, lit by old-fashioned but warm gaslight, were the comfortable walls of the doctor's study and three men hovering about my brother: Seward, Harker, and the madman professor. Their faces were in turn dour, embarrassed, and eager. I could see by the mirror near the terrace doors, my brother's face was pale and hollow.

"Or take her away. Remove her."

The doctor was confused. "Take who away?" asked Seward.

There was no sign of either Mrs. Harker or the distinguished tenant of Carfax. No sooner had I made this observation did my brother look up into the mirror. My face was clear to him, one so accustomed to the dark. His eyes grew wide as they met mine.

"I didn't say anything!"

The three gentlemen whirled around to look out onto the terrace as my brother shrieked over and over of loyalty. There, a common bat — lost in the light — foolishly drew their frantic attention. I moved my back to the door as my brother crouched and gibbered into his hands. The men lost their patience.

"Damn it, Renfield, tell us about Dracula!" shouted the professor. In the hall, I quietly gathered my shoes.

"Dracula?" my brother said, sounding almost sane in his confusion. "I don't know the name."

The professor's questions grew fainter as I carried my shoes and made my silent way down the cold, tile hall.

"Will you let God damn your soul, for the shedding of innocent blood?"

"Oh," my brother said, mournfully, "it is not God who damns me."

I went for a walk.

T he end began when I frightened a child. I recalled only later the whispered promises of chocolates pouring from my lips like vapor as I drew my instruments. I am outside myself in those times, a mystery to myself, but the sensation had never bothered me before. The girl started to cry, the needle too large and sharp at her young throat, and I fled. In fleeing, I observed I was still in my white nurses' uniform, now speckled with little red beads of blood like rat eyes, the arterial spray of my failed gatherings. I hid in a churchyard until just before dawn. I did not like the look of myself as I walked to the Sanitarium and drew the eyes of a few passersby — but I feared no repercussion: it is only deviants who wander the streets at such early hours.

Which was why I was surprised to encounter Mrs. Harker as I attempted to enter the hospital. I stood at the doors, unable to speak, sure she would comment on my appearance. But the lady seemed dazed, her focus turned inward, as she asked to see Dr. Seward. The sudden rattle of an old-fashioned carriage stirred my senses. It did not approach, only moved on, the horses clopping gently away through the still morning, stopping just out of sight. I noted Mrs. Harker's automobile was nowhere in sight.

As I watched the carriage go, Mrs. Harker fluffed the silver-pointed fur collar of her lamb's wool coat, corrected the angle of the small hat on her untidy hair. After a moment's hesitation, she asked, "Have you any experience with women's troubles?" She seemed to regret it immediately, hastily adding, "Sleepwalking. Bad dreams."

They were very different conditions, ma'am.

"Never mind," she snapped, and left in a hurry in the direction of the carriage. She never noticed the blood. The wealthy see very little that does not affect their evenings. Careless creatures for which no door is locked, by day or night.

Papers reported the crying child and mania spilled onto the streets. Just like in our village, rumors began to spread. A white figure roaming the night; mysterious deaths; the grave of a young woman desecrated. Someone was to blame. It couldn't possibly be someone local. Just like the good women of good men could never be unfaithful, monsters would first fly through the air. And no man of wealth and academia could ever be mad — eccentric, perhaps — but lunacy was for another breed. For the poor, the destitute, for young men who had gone abroad and witnessed the wastelands of Europe, death hung rotting upon barbed wire and caught in the teeth of a gunner's nest. It was their responsibility, and their inability to cope. Faults all their own. Like my brother was unable to take responsibility for himself. Not the terror of a night thrown about the hull of a storm-wrecked ship of cadavers, not undiagnosed, late-onset *dementia praecox*. Something catching — or from having been caught, through irresponsibility, through carelessness. Perhaps all these wrongs were something that might be spread with filthy, ill hands, like a fly dancing on a clean white plate. This was not the way of the locals, it had to be something diseased and from afar. Something or someone foreign, with a powerful allure and something to hide.

Someone was to blame.

I was filling charts when I saw Mr. Harker, followed by the professor, storm inside my brother's room. Voices were raised, an argument broke out. I could hear my brother screaming, pleading, as Harker shouted, "What do you know! Madman, what do you know!" I stood to follow as Dr. Seward ran from his office, my brother screaming in strangled burst, when suddenly the shouting stopped with a horrible crack.

Seward and I arrived at my brother's door. Mr. Harker and the professor stood at the far side of the bed, staring to the floor. Harker looked swiftly up as Dr. Seward entered. He looked like a terrified child, face ashen but for his burning forehead, his arms slightly outstretched at his sides like a frightened creature bound to fly.

"We only ... just arrived," he said.

"I heard shouting," said the doctor.

"She ..." Harker licked his dry lips. "She and the Count ... They've gone away. The professor said Renfield knew ..." His moustache twitched over an incredulous, unwell smile. "I only wished to ask ... He got out of hand."

A dark, liquid shadow crept across the floor from the other side of the bed. Dr. Seward brushed by me aside in his haste to enter. "What happened?"

The solicitor's mouth opened and closed but he could not explain. The professor, face keen, launched into a sermon of ill deeds, the stolen innocence of women, the curse of the foreigner, justice done! Dr. Seward shouted for him to be quiet as Harker muttered on and on, pacing before the window as my brother bled out his reputation, his business, his good name on the floor. They would not leave, and they could not help.

I have only ever been helpful.

I spoke loudly. The fighting men fell silent and looked at me. I cleared my throat. I wove the threads of their tales together, braiding for them the rope they needed to clutch in this storm and to save themselves. Or hang from. It made no difference to me.

I described an intruder as they needed: tall and dark and preternaturally powerful who then vanished like a bat through a mist. They all agreed to this story, salivating over the details like hungry dogs. With the soles of their shoes still sticky, they left to pursue their greater foe, their prey, and I was left alone with the body on the floor.

The head bleeds ferociously, but often it exaggerates. More nurses appeared at the door as the gentlemen left. I asked for my tools then dismissed the girls. A few quick stitches, a press of gauze, a quick wrap.

It was time to remove my patient.

I fetched a wheeled chair and spread a wool blanket upon his lap. Down the hall, orderlies nodded as we passed. Out the door and on the grounds, visitors took no notice of another nurse and patient. I strolled to the edge of the lawns and sat behind the hedgerow. He woke soon after, and we waited in silence for dusk. We left, with some effort, through the front gates, my brother's arm around my shoulders. The night gathered us close, concealed us, as I led the way down the narrow streets.

I was at work the next morning. The suspicious orderly noted the runaway — but with the doctor gone, no one ever asked further. No police were ever called, not even when the doctor returned from his abrupt trip to central Europe. My brother's departure was presumed final and, in the light of terrible rumors accompanying the doctor home, an irrelevant element in a ghastly story best forgotten — or at least misremembered. Death is, after all, a common affair at any hospital; no need to tarnish a gentleman with circumstances. I wrote to our parents, informing them that their son was missing, presumed dead.

They have never written back.

T he worst of the scandal made the rounds, though a great deal of fantasy has been sewn within the fabric of the tale, so I hear. The tenant of Carfax's abrupt return to the continent and what happened there — they say it is better left unsaid. The dismissal of the mad professor from various academic institutions, and his rambling writings thereafter. Mrs. Harker treated for melancholy and at the urging of Dr. Seward, she and Mr. Harker sojourned to the mountains for a change of air; they returned five months later with a healthy baby girl. They say it is a beautiful child with raven hair and knowing eyes.

But I do not have time for gossip. My hours are too full.

By day, I work. An angel, I've been called, walking the corridors, white and soft as gossamer. The care my patients receive is that of the highest quality, such that even when one passes, it is remarked that their demeanor is of one who has drifted into a deep and bloodless sleep. I put in a full day, and then come home to the sound of the radio.

I leave it on always. The neighbors have never complained of the cheerful noise. I unpack my bag and place the small, full phials on the dining room table — the large white bedsheet covering it to the floor like a small, stable tent, the chairs of the set placed back by the walls — and rap my fingers on the tabletop. I store my instruments in the deep pockets of my walking coat before I make dinner. I like to keep a neat house.

By night, strangers whisper my name without ever having learned it and tell stories to wayward children of what happens in the dark. I hear them through their open windows, cuddled close to their warm hearths and lamps too reluctantly snuffed out. Tonight, I pass these windows by, my sights set on something greater.

At the Harkers' townhouse, a light remains on downstairs. Most nights, there is little talk here; there is little left to say. Most nights, she goes upstairs unaccompanied. Some nights there is infant crying and lullabies from the nursery, some nights the crying is from elsewhere. On those nights, he stands on the terrace, face turned to the cold sky, the red ember of a cigarette burning like a wicked, knowing eye tight between his fingers. Rare nights, like tonight, he takes to the dark street to wander, hands in his pockets, with his thoughts alone.

There is a dark fog between us, and my footsteps are light.

I walk.

# Renfield, M.E.

## By John Kiste

*Many souls embrace compliance*
*And discredit erudition;*
*I would fain follow bad science*
*Than unblemished superstition.*
*— C. Ucalard*

We have need of a pathologist, as you can see," noted the first constable at the riverbank. "Who is on duty?"

"Renfield," said the second constable.

"Shit!" replied the first.

Two Charing Cross orderlies wheeled the creaking gurney into the dimly lit examination room. The bright bulbs used during autopsies were off, and Medical Examiner Renfield sat casually in one dark corner, munching blow flies from a large snuffbox. The orderlies transferred the sheeted corpse to the examining table, shot disgusted looks into the gloom, and left without a word.

Renfield dabbed his lips with a silk pocket handkerchief, smoothed his tangle of jet black hair and his Penworth vest, and arose and donned a lab coat. He approached the table, switched on the overheads, flooding the area with brilliant light, and threw back the sheet. Involuntarily he sucked air through his teeth.

The corpse appeared to be a middle-aged man with sandy hair and a once-hearty build, but all proof of vitality had dissipated. The body was sunken and shriveled, and the face had been reduced to a hollow stretch of wasp paper skin adhering to the outlines of the skull. Further inspection revealed a caved-in purple chest, ragged nails, and bruised knees, but the rest of the body was as pale as putty. Two raw puncture marks stood out near the throat's carotid artery.

**P**rofessor Abraham Van Helsinki rarely had the opportunity to hear a ringing telephone, so when the candlestick model on the desk of his hotel room began to chime, it took him some seconds to identify the sound. At length he picked up the receiver and heard the operator at the multiplex switchboard announce the call.

"Ah, Renfield, my boy," he replied at length. "Yes, I am still in London. What? Where? Incredible. You were correct to call. I shall be there within the hour."

**T**wo hospital interns lounged and smoked outside the morgue. They had just watched the stooped and wizened figure of Professor Van Helsinki bow his white mane of hair to them and disappear within.

The older trainee nudged the younger. "He's that Dutch specialist that I mentioned before. Comes across when there's a strange or unusual body that stumps the coppers and defies explanation, which happens more often than you might think. May be almost the Twentieth Century, but The Great Wen is still a weird city."

The younger gent was quite new. He seemed puzzled. "And this professor's willing to work with the likes of that 'un?"

"Aye," nodded the veteran. "Whatever you may have heard of his habits, Renfield is the best medical examiner in this Lieutenancy. Mr. Creepy can catch a whiff of poison that any other pathologist would overlook. And he can state to the hour how long the worms have been at a body. Knows death like you know snooker. Just don't eat lunch with him. He's an insectivore."

The other gulped. "I heard. I guess a chocolate-covered cricket diet isn't grounds for dismissal."

Both chuckled as they crushed out their smokes and left the corridor.

Inside, Van Helsinki was bent over the corpse, peering at the punctures in the neck with a gigantic magnifying glass. He turned to Renfield, who stood some yards away in a lab coat now mottled with blood. "And you are certain he has been exsanguinated?"

Renfield nodded. "I just completed the postmortem. The blood on me is literally all there was."

"Who is he?"

"Scotland Yard is working with the constabulary to sort that out. They have his clothes, which I believe they said contained a wallet. The body was found near West Pier on the riverbank."

At that moment, the door burst open and burly Chief Inspector Morris Quince of the Yard lumbered into the morgue. He surveyed the scene. "Professor Van Helsinki," he grunted. "I am glad you are here. Haven't returned home since aiding with those northside rippings, eh? Well this case needs you more. The identification confirms our body is none other than the Honorable Lord Godarnett. This ups the stakes in the eyes of the Commissioner. I have the Lord's friend Dr. Jack Sewer of Carfax Sanitarium on his way over to positively identify the corpse. What have you learned?"

Van Helsinki stroked his steel gray mustache. "It is a most curious case, Inspector. Give us a bit more time to organize our findings."

"Well, be quick about it." Quince turned his pudgy face to Renfield, and his eyes nearly vanished in the folds of his frown as he pointed at the pathologist. "And you! For Gawd's sake, try not to be a damn loony while we investigate this. You made the Commissioner throw up last month when he walked in on your snacking. By Christ, try to *act* human, anyway."

Renfield pulled out his gold pocket watch and stared at it.

"Gad!" snapped Quince and rushed out.

Van Helsinki was still smiling when Dr. Sewer arrived. The head of the local sanitarium (i.e. asylum, i.e. madhouse), he was tall and lanky with dark features and damp cheeks. He gasped at the state of the body and at the face that was barely a face.

"The sandy hair helps, not a lot else. But it's definitely Godarnett. Was he drained of blood?"

Renfield nodded.

"By what?"

"We are still working on that," said Renfield quietly.

Sewer turned to the professor. "Van Helsinki. It is good to see you again, though not under these circumstances. We shall no doubt require your wisdom and expertise. Lord Godarnett's best friends, Jonathan Heckler and his wife Mynah, are staying with me at the sanitarium. I refused to let them come witness this, but we all desire explanations. Could you gentlemen join us for dinner, say around eight o'clock?"

Renfield hesitated, but Van Helsinki bowed. "We would be honored, Jack."

The professor and the pathologist exited a hansom cab at Carfax asylum just as distant Big Ben sounded the hour. They were led by a servant through several dark hallways at the front of the massive complex and were warmly greeted as they entered a long, oak-paneled Georgian dining hall lit by an exquisite chandelier of immense proportions. Sewer led them past servants and down a sort of impromptu receiving line to introduce the other guests.

Renfield shifted uncomfortably in his tuxedo and pulled at his bow tie. A tall handsome youth shook his hand and then gestured to a stunning auburn-haired girl next to him wearing a shimmering green velvet evening dress. "I am Jonathan Heckler," the youth said, "and this is my wife Mynah. And here..." he further gestured to a lithe blonde in an impeccable pearl-studded ensemble, "is my wife's best friend, Lucy Westengurl."

"My great pleasure," mumbled Renfield.

Fifteen minutes of mindless chatter with overtones of loss and terror regarding their friend's death preceded dinner, but at length all were ushered to their chairs. A sumptuous steak and fish repast ensued, with Van Helsinki requesting seconds of each and Renfield politely eschewing every course. He insisted he had no appetite, but it was clear that a fly's gossamer wing clung to the lower corner of his lip. Indeed, at one point, Lucy Westengurl, who had been seated next to him, not too discreetly slid to the next empty chair and noisily dragged her plate and silverware along with her.

By dessert, the conversation turned in earnest to the killing. Heckler asked the professor his thoughts. Van Helsinki smiled knowingly. "As you may have observed," he said, "I have brought along my doctor's bag. Presently I shall present the contents and give you my theory. Hmm? What say you, Jack?"

Sewer appeared preoccupied. He looked up, startled. "Renfield," he queried, "where was the body found?"

"Just south of here — a stone's throw, in fact. By the river. Why?"

"This is disturbing in a new way." Jack stroked his chin. "Might it have been seen from the sanitarium's fourth floor rear windows?"

Renfield nodded. "Certainly possible. Again, why?"

"Gentlemen — and ladies — a most disturbed patient named Swills is in a padded cell at the rear of the fourth floor. There is, however, a barred window well off the floor that he might have endeavored to reach..."

"And...?" Heckler anxiously dragged out the word.

"The orderly on four told me Swills was hysterical about seeing something black and 'fluttery' outside attacking a *gentleman*. He was so maniacal about it that at length I gave him a strong sedative and ordered the staff not to disturb his sleep. Perhaps there was more to his ravings than I originally thought."

"Possibly," mused Van Helsinki.

Sewer checked his pocket watch. "He should be waking soon. I shall go up and see if he is lucid. If he *is* coherent, may I come get you gentlemen?"

"Absolutely!" barked Van Helsinki. "Don't waste a minute."

Sewer tossed down his napkin and hurried from the dining hall. No one spoke for some minutes. Then Mynah Heckler took a long draught of after dinner champagne. "My! Did he say something black and 'fluttery'?"

Lucy laughed. "But the patient is a lunatic. Literally."

"Perhaps," enjoined the professor. "But do not rule out the possibility that this account may actually be tied to our investigation."

"I hear the police are stumped," said Heckler. "But not you, professor?"

"Maybe not, my young friend. I have a hypothesis, to be sure. What do you think, Renfield?"

Renfield slightly shrugged. "The case is certainly odd."

Under her breath, Lucy Westengurl muttered, "And *you* would know odd, mate."

At that moment, a muffled gunshot sounded from somewhere in the rear of the estate.

All leapt to their feet. Mynah's champagne flute shattered on the floor. Everyone started toward the corridor, but

Heckler waved the ladies back. A bearded coachman who had clearly heard the shot ran past the doorway. Heckler buttonholed him and ordered him to send for the police and then remain with the women. He, Van Helsinki, and Renfield made their way into the depths of the mansion. Heckler was familiar with the asylum and led them to the doorway where the living quarters merged with the hospital. Beyond this, the floors were laid with tiles and the dirty walls were painted seafoam green.

They found the stairwell and climbed to the fourth floor. Here in the long hallway they discovered two nurses and several attendants ministering to an ashen Jack Sewer, who sat upon the floor next to an open iron door. Behind other closed doors, patients were wailing and laughing and hooting, but no sound came from the open room. As they reached Jack, he held out a small revolver to Van Helsinki that smelled of gunpowder.

Renfield and Heckler pushed past through the opening. There, on the padded floor of the small cell, lay a man with one arm extending from a straitjacket, his shiny fingernails curved into a claw, and most of his face blown away. Brains oozed from his dark blonde hair and blood radiated across the cushioned floor and spattered the small mattress and the puffy cork-crumb-filled canvas walls. What remained of the chin was black with powder burns. Renfield noted to himself that the barred window was high up the rear wall, but could potentially be reached once the straitjacket was breached. Observation of the river was a possibility.

"What happened, Jack?" he heard Van Helsinki ask and returned to the doorway.

Sewer composed himself and waved the attendants away. He pointed to the small revolver. "I always carry that in my coat. Even with orderlies close, I feel more secure in some cells if I have it. As a last resort, mind you. Never even thought of it in this case. Damn Swills! No one was to go near his cell. He was heavily sedated. I guess not heavily enough. I deemed it safe to go in alone as he was lying in bed. I never noticed he had worked free of the straitjacket. He was on me before I could summon help, raving that the black demon was coming to get *him* next. Either he had somehow heard of my revolver, or felt it in my lower coat pocket, for he had clutched it in an instant. I caught his hand just as it cleared the pocket, and it immediately went off. He had found the trigger and inadvertently done himself in. I was stunned, but I truly don't believe he wanted the weapon to use on me. Something had scared him mightily. Something unearthly. You should have seen his eyes. Whatever he had seen, he believed in its evil. Of that I am sure. Have you alerted the police? Better get Quince here."

Orderlies returned to guard the cell until the police arrived and the party started back for the dining hall. Renfield split from the group and entered a windowed doorway farther down the hall. No one missed him. No one ever did. The gray chamber was Sewer's private operating room. Renfield had realized as much. Through the window he had seen the glass jars of leeches and maggots on a counter. Leeches were no longer used for the passe procedure of bloodletting, but they were still infrequently employed to encourage blood flow in patients' extremities, and maggots still aided in the elimination of necrotic tissue.

The pathologist was uncomfortable taking such advantage of his host. He himself despised being an insectivore, but any other food made him violently ill — and the jar's occupants looked so fresh. He lifted the metal lids and scooped a fair handful of each into his mouth. The creatures were so delicate but so full of life. And God, how they squirmed.

He pulled his handkerchief from his tuxedo pocket as he wandered about the lab equipment, munching contentedly. He was curious about the varied medical pieces; they were so much more expensive than his own morgue accoutrements. He touched razor sharp scalpels longingly, and ran his thumb across the blade of a costly bone saw. He scanned shelves of rare chemical compounds, and probed racks of Erlenmeyer flasks and pored over strange delicate pumps fitted with rubber tubing.

This rubber tubing fascinated him; thin red drops ran from its mouth. He scooped another fistful of leeches from the jar and crossed the room to inspect a brand-new Zeiss microscope.

When Renfield reentered the dining room, Inspector Quince and a uniformed constable had joined the party. Dr. Sewer was again recounting Swills's death, stressing in the strongest terms that whatever the mental patient had seen from his cell window fluttering around Lord Godarnett on the riverbank had petrified him with an unreasoning terror.

Quince took it all in, casting glances at the other faces in the room as he did. The women were in a near panic, and Heckler was biting his nails, but Professor Van Helsinki looked calm and all-knowing, almost smug. He tapped on his bag, and the inspector yielded the floor.

"It is time to put the puzzle pieces together, to use our knowledge and our senses to glean the truth." Van Helsinki unclasped his leather bag.

"What we are dealing with, my friends, as incredible as it sounds, is a vampire."

"Vampire?" gasped Mynah and Lucy.

"Yes. The Nosferatu. The Undead. A bloodsucking beast who may even now be targeting Lord Godarnett's friends. We must prepare ourselves." As the others looked on in abject horror, Van Helsinki began to empty his surgeon's bag of garlic, crosses, wooden stakes, mallets, and vials of holy water.

Renfield interrupted him. "What we are dealing with is simple, commonplace murder, albeit cleverly pulled off. Isn't that right, Jack?"

Dr. Sewer's mouth fell open. "What?"

Everyone was now staring at the strange little medical examiner. He went on. "I am given to believe your original intentions were altruistic. I saw your lab equipment. Your experiments dealt with improving blood transfusions to make them safer and more efficient. Naturally you eventually needed a human test subject. You chose poor hapless Swills, who was hardly in a position to argue, and conducted your trials in secret. You didn't bother to learn of his anemia and his leukocytosis, but it was *his* blood I found in the tubes of your transfusion equipment, with its overabundance of white blood cells and its sad dearth of red ones. He was not a strong candidate, and at some point he died on your table. Now you were in a pickle, doctor, because you couldn't let a patient be found dead from blood loss. Suspicion would fall on no one else."

"This is crazy," stammered Sewer. "You all know Swills accidentally shot himself."

"Not so, Jack," cut in Renfield. "That's what you needed us to think. You couldn't just drain the rest of Swills's blood via puncture wounds in his throat. You would still be suspected. He had to be found outside the sanitarium. And he had to become someone else. You needed a *new* Swills. Then you remembered your friend Lord Godarnett had sandy, dark blond hair as well, and nearly the same build. You privately invited your friend here, and sad to say, you did away with him too, probably by a blow to the face that you knew would be later obliterated. Somehow you got his body into Swills's cell, switched their clothes, and left Swills with the Lord's identification near the Thames, after giving orders that Swills's cell was not to be disturbed because you had been forced to sedate him. Now this evening you staged that little scene for us, remarking that Swills had been anxious because he knew something of the unearthly murder, and you popped off to his cell and blew the face off Lord Godarnett's corpse, rendering it unrecognizable."

"My God Jack!" cried Heckler.

"This is insane!" shrieked Sewer, but Quince had now taken up a position behind him.

"I am afraid not," continued the little pathologist. "You were the one who came to identify the shriveled, exsanguinated corpse at the morgue, without allowing the Hecklers to see it. Even though it was *that* corpse's blood that matched the anemic blood in your transfusion equipment upstairs. I just made the comparison with that gorgeous new microscope of yours.

"Furthermore, that corpse had the ragged fingernails of a mental patient, while the faceless fake Swills you presented us had the shiny manicured nails of the upper class. And finally, the powder burns on faux Swills's chin would not have been so pronounced if the small gun had been fired from the hip, as you claimed.

"Oh, by the way, I talked to the orderly on four before coming down. *He* never informed you of Swills's fears, as you told us. He said you had simply told him the patient was sedated and not to be disturbed. I suppose you thought your account would never be questioned. Perhaps with a good barrister, you can end your days as an inmate of your own asylum, and not as a customer of Gallow's Hill."

Quince placed his hand on Sewer's shoulder and the doctor went limp at the touch. "You little fly eater," he sighed resignedly. "I could have developed techniques and methods to save countless thousands of lives. Let their blood be on your hands."

A constable cuffed bracelets onto Sewer's hands and he was led from the asylum.

Embarrassed, Van Helsinki began putting stakes and mallets back into his leather bag. Jonathan Heckler stared from his wife to Renfield, who casually plucked a fat spider from the door jamb and put it between his teeth. Lucy Westengurl gagged and ran swearing from the room.

Van Helsinki smiled. "And you were doing so well, my boy," he said.

**John Kiste** is a horror writer who was previously the president of the Stark County Convention & Visitors' Bureau and a board member of the Massillon Museum. He is a double-lung transplantee and organ donation ambassador, a McKinley Museum planetarian and an Edgar Allan Poe impersonator who has been published in Flame Tree Press's Terrifying Ghosts, Third Flatiron, Madhouse Books, Dark Recesses Press, Hiraeth Books, A Shadow of Autumn, and dozens of other anthologies, magazines, and e-zines. He recently won The Dark Sire Award for Best Fiction. You can find him at johnkiste.wordpress.com.

# The Spider Logs

## By Emma Kathryn

*The following log was found aboard a light craft called the* Spider *— a vessel mostly used for ferrying supplies between space stations and troubled vessels.*

*All crew, save for Pilot Renfield, who was found attempting to hide in the ship's ventilation system, are dead. No other living soul was found, nor did we find evidence of the creature Renfield refers to in the following files. It appears she began her entries immediately after the death of the crew. None of the captain's logs prior to this have anything untoward in them. In fact, we believe some of the captain's logs may have been deleted, but we are currently unsure as to why.*

*None of the crew are named in Renfield's version of events. We are unsure as to why she has chosen to do this as they clearly worked together long enough for her to know them all well. Details on the identities of the rest of the crew are available upon request but we did not feel necessary to include in this document.*

*We have absolutely no idea how one single woman managed to cause as much carnage as she has and these files have been taken into review as part of the Holmwood Inquiry.*

*Pilot Renfield has been referred for immediate psychiatric treatment and has been taken into custody by the authorities.*

<u>Entry #1</u>

I have made a pact with the thing in the vents. We are not friends; we are not enemies. It is simply a gentleman's agreement between woman and beast. I find it food; it doesn't eat me. We both survive. Simple.

The rest of the crew is gone. All three of them.

It was likely the medic's fault. Or, at least, that's what I've managed to convince myself. We collected a sealed box from the *Seward*, a medical carrier that we swung by. They told us it held samples that were to be taken to Whitby Space Station for immediate shipment to Earth.

I found her in the med bay, strung up by black tendrils. They were in her eyes, her nostrils, her ears and her mouth, holding her high into the air, only inches away from the ceiling. Beneath her jerking feet, lay the box from the *Seward*, open and with the lid broken off. Black fluid poured out of it and spilled to the floor. The thing that was slowly devouring her was a constantly moving mass of black veins and tendons. The medic gargled and choked past the snaking tubes entering her body and her fingers twitched in my direction.

I stepped out and locked the door behind me, leaving the beast to eat our doctor. For hours after, I hid myself in the cockpit, sweating and shaking and trying to forget what I'd seen. The Captain came by later and asked if I'd seen the medic. They had found her shoes and her jumpsuit locked in the med bay but couldn't find her. I shook my head and she left me to my charts and buttons and gears.

Nobody found her and nobody suggested there was something wild on the loose on the ship. That night, the medic's ID badge was sitting on my pillow. Something knew what I'd done. A vent above my head rattled in appreciation. Sometimes, I thought I heard whispering. I didn't sleep that night.

Three days later it was the mechanic. I'd spent the morning keeping as far away from the walls as possible, dodging anything that a tendril could slip out of. When I got to the cockpit, a warning light was flashing and the mechanic didn't answer when I radioed.

I went down to the engine room to find her. Between pipes and cannisters, she hid with a fire extinguisher, blasting at anything that came near. She'd seen it and it had driven her mad almost immediately. I glanced around and saw wiry black fingers sliding over hot, steaming pipes. It was coming. Lying to the mechanic, I told her it was fine and took her hand. More whispering met my ears. It was giving me the chance to live. I had to take it. I threw her to the mass of writhing blackness and ran.

The Captain started to panic after that. For about a week, it was just her and I. She sent out mayday call after mayday call but I knew none of it would help. It had asked me to shut off the comms. Just until the Captain was gone. She strode up and down the hallways of our little ship, screaming at the walls. Sometimes, I wondered if the creature had spoken to her and she'd refused its offer. It didn't matter. When she came to tell me that we needed to go back to the *Seward*, it got her. It had been waiting with me in the cockpit, knowing that she'd think the best thing would be to stay together. I watched this time. I didn't look away.

Now it's just the beast and me. Floating through the stars.


Entry #2


I've stopped keeping track of the days. I don't need them anymore. Instead, I just keep track of my rations and fuel. The beast still promises not to eat me but we'll both be getting hungry soon. I knew we would need to find another ship. A little one. Not the kind that will find me alone and cart me off to the madhouse.

There was nothing on my radar for miles but the creature squatted in the air vent above me and whispered co-ordinates to me. Its senses are much better than my machines and I obeyed.

We found a small cargo ship not long later. I marveled at the monster's tracking skills and tried to work out how it knew where they were. This was amazing. The ship was the *Quincey*, an American cargo ship, which dragged rocks across the skies. A tiny ping of my distress beacon and they came like flies to honey. There were five of them. These weren't good numbers. They could easily alert a security vessel or even send messages to the Whitby. I'd be on a prison colony in no time.

For a moment, it sounded as though the creature was laughing at me. *If you want to survive longer, you will have to grow claws*, it told me.

Three came aboard and we made short work of them. I killed a man. For the first time in my life. I stabbed him with a scalpel from the medical bay and watched him bleed. I didn't expect there to be so much mess. The creature killed the other two, wrapping them tightly in its black tentacles. For a fleeting second, I thought that it had grown since I'd first seen it, but I was too distracted by all the blood from the man. So much blood. Just… so…much…

The beast reminded me that there was no time for that right now and we radioed the *Quincey*, telling them they were good to board. The remaining two crewmates sounded surprised and came over to see what had become of their colleagues.

I killed them both. The beast hissed that it was proud of me. It let me board the Quincey and take whatever I needed. "What of the bodies?" I asked aloud. *They are nothing to worry about*, the beast promised.

Scavenging the *Quincey* took longer than I thought. It was like having a holiday in someone else's house. I took sensible things like food and fuel cannisters and first aid. But then I went to their dorms and began collecting trinkets.

Photographs of children, jewelry, books, hairbrushes, an empty matchbook from a bar on Earth, army dog tags, a tiny plastic plant…

When I returned, the bodies were indeed gone. But the blood remained. *You must do your share*, the beast whispered. So, I did.

I have been mopping up blood for longer than I care to think. I've stopped counting days so who really knows?

*Investigator's note: the* Quincey *has been located and its crew all reported missing. All of the items noted in the log were found on the* Spider. *Family members of the missing have identified some of these as belonging to their loved ones.*


Entry #3


The next couple were easy. We'd been targeting the occasional pleasure boat. The most recent was some rich Earth tourist with too much money and not enough sense. I actually enjoyed killing him. The beast ate his two assistants. We didn't get much fuel from him, but I did manage to take some good stuff from his quarters.

Designer clothes and an expensive watch. Sometimes I wear them on our ship and pretend I'm fancy. He also had lots of video games, so I obviously took them, too. I've been amusing myself with them on our trips between targets. Some of them are fun.

They are also incredibly distracting and taking up a lot of my time. I guess that's a good thing. It means I don't focus on how long we've been alone out here.

Anyway, I have a high score to beat.


Entry #4


This one was stupid. We shouldn't have done this.

After the tourists, it was a British government supply ship. The *Holmwood*. That was our biggest one. It had twelve people. Twelve people and them all being British government felt risky. But we were both so hungry. The last tourist's ship hadn't been enough. The beast promised that if we did this, we wouldn't have to worry about finding anyone else for a long time.

The beast somehow managed to kill their comms once I had spoken to them though. Part of me was confused by this. Why couldn't it do that on our own ship back when the Captain was trying to send out mayday calls? It told me that I had taught it how to do this and that I should be proud. Like it was proud of me after we took down the American ship.

I've been noticing that I've been changing too. I'm getting better at climbing and slipping into small spaces. Sometimes, when we're on a ship, I can hide in the vents just as easily as the beast can. I can slither into shadows and strike without someone knowing I'm there. I don't think about anything when I'm like this, I just listen to the beast talking in my head, telling me when to strike. It can see and feel everything so no-one can ever hide from it.

Killing twelve people was exhausting. We couldn't stop either. We had to get them all as quickly as possible. Comms were down but who knows what these sneaky government buggers might have as back-up. I don't know how many I took out and how many the beast did but when we knew they were all dealt with, I collapsed and fell asleep on their ship, right amongst all the blood and the bodies.

There's always so much blood now. I see it in my dreams.

When I woke, the beast told me I'd done well. This was it — we didn't have to find any more ships for ages now. We were free to live off of all of this for as long as we saw fit. I nodded and set about gathering supplies, fuel, and trinkets.

The beast doesn't whisper any more. It just talks. It has a voice as loud as mine. None of the people on the other ships ever hear it, just me. We talk like we've known each other our whole lives. When we're out on a ship, all our talk is of directions and orders and warnings. When we're on our own little boat, it's stories and places we could go and people I knew back home.

It has started suggesting that I call it Master. Instead of simply the beast or the creature or the thing. I don't really see why not. Although it does seem strange. I thought we were equal in all this, but on days like today, when we have destroyed a vessel of this size, I am reminded of how easily this fly could be picked off of the web and eaten for dinner.

However, I'm much too tired to worry about this just now. I may sleep for an eternity.

*Investigator's note: the* Holmwood *has been located and, again, all of its crew are missing. This ship's disappearance was reported shortly after their communication systems went down. This confirms the basic facts of Renfield's version of events but we are still at a loss as to how she killed all crew on board and where the bodies are. It has been suggested that she disposed of them out of the airlock but we have absolutely no evidence of this.*

<u>Entry #5</u>

Master says it is time again. I am angry. The *Holmwood* was supposed to last us much longer than this. I still have plenty of my supplies and we've got enough fuel to get us halfway to Earth. This is madness.

Master doesn't always stay in the vents anymore. It likes to take up space in the engine room, where it hides its own gory stock and supplies. I don't know how it keeps the bodies fresh. Surely, they would all have rotted fairly quickly? Or maybe, it never gives things enough time to rot and I just don't notice? I don't bare to think about it sometimes.

My own collection has grown a bit manic. My trinkets and trophies and toys have spread from my dorm over to the cold and empty rooms of my former shipmates. They don't mind. They are dead after all. Sometimes, I lie on one of their empty beds and look up at the walls. I've covered them with stolen pictures and art and, after one exceptionally lucky find, some fairy lights. I wrap myself in reclaimed blankets, knitted by mothers or lovers or bored hobbyists, and make myself a little nest of pilfered shit. It makes me feel safe and horrid at the same time.

After Master started suggesting that we find our next target, I've started my own project. I sit and flick through hundreds of different radio stations and comms channels, trying to find if anyone has been reporting our activities. It has become my new obsession.

White noise has become my new enemy. The static crackle between channels fills me with dread as I anticipate that the next voice that I hear will be heralding my doom. At least two different channels have started asking others about the *Holmwood*. People are looking for it, which means people are looking for us.

When I put this to the Master, it tried to dismiss me and told me there's nothing to worry about. But all I do now is worry. I argued back. Voices raised. My chest puffed up and the Master grew the biggest I've ever seen it. It's now the entire height of the room, with veins and tendrils pushing against the ceiling and the walls when it's full size. It could crush me and drink my insides at any moment. But just now my anger is stronger than the image of the medic with all her orifices stuffed with tentacles.

I told it we were being reckless and should keep our heads down for longer. It warned me it was hungry and I should remember my place. Screams welled up in me but I fought them down. I managed to very calmly say, "You can't pilot this ship without me".

The Master fills my head with its words. "I could drink you and wait for the rescue crew," it says.

"If they ever find us," I say. "I've been very good at keeping us below everyone's radar"

There's silence. It's the first time in eons that I've heard nothing but quiet. Bliss fills my head and, even if only for a moment, it's beautiful.

"That's what I thought," I said and stormed off to the mechanic's old bunk. I put on a pair of headphones and I've been listening to filched Earth music ever since. Someone on the *Holmwood* had good taste in tunes.


<u>Entry #6</u>


The Master woke me with a cacophony of smashing. It had trashed my own dorm. A warning of what could have happened if I'd been sleeping in there and hadn't nodded off in the mechanic's quarters.

"We're going to Whitby Space Station," it told me.

I guess we're going to Whitby then.

I am sitting in the cockpit, plotting a course to Whitby. Whenever I think it's not looking, I go back to surfing the communication channels.

They know that the *Holmwood* is a mausoleum now. They'll be coming for us soon.


*Investigator's note: looking at the pilot's charts and the start of her travels to Whitby, we can see those communications about the Holmwood's disappearance coincide with her comments.*


<u>Entry #7</u>


We are nearing Whitby. I don't know what I am more frightened of anymore. The Master or the people hunting the killers of the *Holmwood*? I have listened to many reports and it even made it on to the public newsfeeds recently. People think a group of trained killers is hunting down ships. It also seems that the tourist was some kind of celebrity so that's added fuel to the fire.

I have spent a lot of time hunkered down amongst my horde in the dormitories. I look at the pictures of the dead people and touch their things. Lockets, stuffed animals, sports trophies. It's not safe here anymore.

The Master only talks to me when it really has to right now. It's still angry that I spoke back. The closer we get to Whitby, the more that I worry that it'll just kill me anyway. Once we're in radar range, it could just decide to feast on my innards.

But at the same time, once we're on radar, the security ships could just come and arrest me. Lock me up and send me off to one of the really awful colonies where they make you smash up Martian rocks until you drop dead. Or maybe they'll get here and just decide to toss me out of the airlock — save themselves the hassle and expense of a trial. Or maybe, when they arrive, the Master will just eat them.

I hate the not knowing, that's what's really killing me. My stomach hurts and I've found myself starting to pull my hair out, strand by strand. Like pulling wings off a fly. I can't stand it anymore. All this constant white noise.

I just wish something would happen.

<u>Entry #8</u>

We're in radar range of Whitby. Time is up. The Master wants me to request to dock. I've worked out what it wants and I don't think I can do it. It was bad enough when it was just a few people. Whitby has at least a hundred and there are ships docking and taking off all the time.

It's the perfect place for chaos.

And I just can't.

My hair is missing in chunks now and I vomit up most of what I eat. I've gone on like this enough.

Today I sent out a mayday call. The Master will learn soon enough. Hell, it might even be exactly what it was hoping I would do.

Now, I'm going to just bunker down in the vent above my cockpit and wait and wait and wait and wait and wait...

*Investigator's note: The Pilot Renfield's medical records report that her hair is missing in chunks and that severe damage to the stomach lining indicates the illness she has described. The frustrating thing about this case is the intertwining of fact and fiction. Our theory is that there was an accomplice who escaped and in during her episode, Renfield turned this other person into a monstrous creature. Further investigation into the ship recommended in an attempt to find evidence of this "Master" she wrote of.*

*End of evidence file.*

**Emma Kathryn** is a horror fanatic from Glasgow, Scotland. When she's not scaring herself to death, she's either podcasting as one half of the Yearbook Committee Podcast or she's streaming indie games on Twitch as variety streamer, girlofgotham.

# The Crushing Weight of an Elephant's Soul

## By Cat Voleur

We are many.

But we are so, very small.

Beings as small as us, we must relish the small victories.

His hand twitches toward where he thinks the buzzing comes from. The echoes of our lives linger there in the window, where we used to crawl. His fingers search there for the sound, not realizing we are still inside him, where he has put us.

The hand comes back empty, having caught nothing. We wait for his anger, for a frenzy, a massacre, a storm that does not come. He just drifts off back to sleep, having eaten no more of our brothers tonight.

It's just one small victory.

But it's the beginning of the end for Renfield.


We used to matter more to him.

We were a prize.

An obsession.

Now he wants a cat.

He asks the very fine young doctor for a kitten. Perhaps he can sense there are nearly enough of us to overwhelm him now. Perhaps he suspects what it is we are up to. He could want something to reign us in — and it might work. We don't know if we could control a cat.

We wait in silence, save for our buzzing.

The doctor stares carefully into Renfield's eyes. He does not see us. No one ever does. We can see him very well, however.

There is curiosity burning in every inch of his expression. He wants to know how long the kitten would last, and what would come after. There is a morbid fascination in this case, and a desire to see it reach its natural conclusion.

Our anticipation manifests in Renfield. We are a nervous flutter in his stomach where we were all laid to rest. He twitches.

He knows even better than we do how many of us there are.

He keeps track.

Four flies per day to a small spider.

Two small spiders to a medium spider.

Four of those to a big spider.

A bird can easily devour three of those big spiders in a day.

There are five birds still alive in the room.

He reckons a kitten could eat as many birds as it is able to catch.

The doctor has looked over all these detailed accounts. He too wants to know how many birds a kitten would be worth, but does not, it seems, want to be responsible for the death of the kitten. Or the puppy that would likely follow.

Puppies and kittens grow into dogs and cats. Pets. They evoke a sympathy that the doctor never showed to any of us.

The request is denied.

For today.

For now.

As he sulks, Renfield crunches more of our brothers between his teeth.

We add their wings and webs to our army.

There is another man.

He is older than the doctor, but just as fine in his manner of speech and dress.

He comes in as we did, through the window.

This man should be the end game. He has devoured several humans, after all, and it puts him one step above what we had considered to be the top of the chain. But it does not seem to work as it should. There are no trapped souls lingering inside him, as we all linger in Renfield.

There is nothing but abyss behind his dark eyes.

He is empty.


The doctor knows something is changing.

He can see Renfield losing interest in us.

The doctor presses him for information now, to study this affliction in its entirety before it is eclipsed by a new madness. The madness of Enoch. Of God. Of souls.

That is what Renfield speaks of now, even as the doctor tries to refocus him. To remind him of us.

The doctor wishes to know the end game.

He wants to know if Renfield would eat a man.

Instead, he asks about what an elephant soul must be like. We can all feel the tremble of fear that such a question inspires.

Our host does not want to know what such a thing would be like — he does not even wish to imagine it. He believes that the weight of an elephant soul would be too heavy to bear. He fears being crushed beneath it.

He does not consider that crushing would be a quick death.

Better one quick crush than to be drowned slowly over time.

We wonder how he does not feel himself already sinking.


Renfield serves the window man now, this Count. He calls him Master.

He has ceased to pay any attention to us.

It means we can move as we please.

But it also means there will be no more brothers coming to join us.

We must move forward with only what we have.

There is something ominous in the Master, this eater of man with no soul behind his eyes.

He promises rewards.

We know what Renfield does not, what his servitude shall really bring him.

Oblivion.

He shall have nothing but unearned silence after his death should his Master eat him.

He would become nothing.

We cannot have that.

We deserve our feast.

Renfield claims that he is cured.

He begs for a release.

For once, we are on the same page as our host. We hope that the doctor believes the ruse.

The Count wants to take Renfield into his service proper.

Obviously, we cannot let such a thing happen.

If his Master feeds on him, his soul will be shredded and condemned to that abyss. After how long we have waited, how patient we have been, it would be nothing short of Hell to see our greatest meal consumed before we have the strength to take it.

On the other hand, if Renfield fails to complete his mission, we shall be robbed of that chance all the sooner.

The Master will come.

He will kill Renfield in his anger, and there will be nothing we can do to stop him.

We will lose our last, fleeting chance to overpower him this next night when he sleeps.

One way or the other, this shall be our last time seeing the doctor.

For once, we are grateful that he cannot see us.

We don't want him to be thinking of sugar, or flies, or spiders or birds. We want him to forget Renfield was ever obsessed with us, that he was ever a mad man.

We need this chance.

We need him to let our host escape.

As quietly as we can, we control our buzzing and await the verdict.

Renfield has failed The Count.

He failed also to escape.

We accept that it's over for us, that we have lost our chance as his Master grips Renfield by the neck in fury.

Then he sees us.

The Master actually sees us through the window of Renfield's eyes.

No one else has ever been aware of our presence. Of our taste for vengeance.

A dark smile crosses over the face of this man who is not a man.

He sees another opportunity for the punishment of failure.

He sees a use for us.

Quietly he asks the question, if we are ready to serve.

We are.

We had accepted defeat at first, but now, we accept him. Our Master.

What could have been the end for all of us is just the beginning as The Count snaps the back of our worthless host and drops him to the floor.

Renfield does not understand why he was not condemned to the sweet abyss, but he is grateful. He lusts for something eternal, for more life, even as his broken body convulses on the floor.

He tries to thank Master.

He tries to apologize.

He can achieve neither of these things, nor ask why his life was spared.

We already know the answer, and he shall find out soon enough.

The Count does not ruin the surprise and does not say a word. He simply smiles and turns back toward the window.

Silently, he leaves Renfield, helpless, to our tender care.

He aches for his Master — our Master — to return.

Our buzzing grows louder.

He is defenseless.

Thousands of us rise up together.

Countless wings.

Eternal legs.

We crawl over and under his measly human soul in our hunger. We feed, at last, as one.

It is better than the flies and spiders.

It is better even than the initial offering of sugar that had lured so many of us in.

He is screaming, twisting as best he can through his paralysis. He gurgles in agony and begs for us to stop.

For someone to make it stop.

How many countless of us did he savor the dying taste of? How many countless were swallowed whole?

We do not heed his cries.

The weight of all of us together is larger and more crushing than any elephant as we bear down upon him.

We are small.

But we are so, very many.

# Zoophagus

## By Jeremy Megargee

I allow the ants to explore my tongue, and when the moment is right, I draw them deeper into the cavern of my gullet, clamping my teeth tight and blackening their world until it is nothing but dark and wet. There's a nutty flavor, and then they fall forever into the pit of me. The appetite is not born of malice, and it is not the result of filling an emotional void, as the prodding psychiatrists would like to claim. It is willing sacrifice.

The insects have a sense of base morality that even the most perceptive men of science fail to realize. They know that I am mortal, and our flesh is weak and fragile to the touch. There's no longevity attached to a human life, only the slow burning of a dimming flame, and if I am to be a match for *him* -- if I am to stand against him -- the insects know that I'll need them.

I'll admit that *he* charmed me in the beginning. He's good at ensnaring in that way, with soft words and gestures to establish trust. And why wouldn't he be a professional at such tactics? He's had thousands of years to practice his subtle manipulations. Draw forth the sycophants, make them feel special, make them feel accepted, and hiss out the occasional promise of immortality or freedom from a house of failing flesh.

I let him take from me. I have allowed him to take from me for longer than I'd like to admit. He has taken pride, self-worth, and blood of the darkest scarlet. Always small meals of plasma, and never enough to grant me that gift that he's always whispering about. This world will teach you that certain entities are takers and never givers. It is better to spot them early and save yourself a lifetime of pain, but I didn't have the means to see what was right in front of me.

I never even noticed those bright yellow wolf's eyes eating me up from beneath a shawl of feigned benevolence. I cooed when he came, and I nuzzled up against his chest like a stupid dog that begs for even a modicum of affection. Those nights of puncture wounds and warm embraces, and how I longed to share words with him, thoughts I'd never told another soul, but he had no want of those. His visitations were brief, inherently selfish. I never saw it then, but now, I can't stop seeing it.

Dracula is a taker, but the vermin are givers, and they have chosen me to be their champion.

T he tarantulas crawl two by two along the windowsill, and for them I am Noah, and they accept the invitation into my Ark. They tickle my throat when I consume them, and protracted fangs kiss my esophagus. The great centipedes follow, legs in the hundreds, and when I slurp them down, I feel strength like iron taking root in my limbs.

There's a smeared looking glass on the wall of my cramped cell, and when I gaze at my own reflection, I see the flies that congregate behind my irises. I am no longer alone.

I am thousands, and the lives that crawl and buzz and skitter in me have taken on symbiotic roles. That cold, everlasting walking death that leaks from Dracula's fangs isn't the only doorway to eternity. He has denied me, so I've discovered a different path.

I think back to how I'd act around him in those early days. I'd plead and supplicate and grant him his every whim. I'd betray my own opinions and be whatever he needed me to be. I wanted so desperately to be loved, and I chose the wrong dead man to love me. People pleasing rots you out from the inside, and when the taker has left, you feel like a husk scraped of an authentic sense of self.

I thought myself ruined for a long time. I'd weep out oceans to stain my single goosefeather pillow. I'd lie on the cot, staring up at the pitted ceiling, and I'd ask why I attract only those that want to drain all the best parts of me out. I naturally assumed that I must be the problem.

But the spiders, the rats, the flies, and the low things of the world told me different. They reminded me that I am a person that deserves respect, and that it's time to make a change.

They told me that *he* has always used them too, and they've grown tired of being used. I've come to believe in karma now. Karma has mandibles, carapaces, and translucent wings. And when provoked, karma drips venom.

My knees have scabs from kneeling before him in midnight hours.

I will kneel no more.

I meet the rats at the little metallic sink in the corner of the cell, and up from the drain they climb, eager explorers, and they find a new nesting place in the soft crevices of my straitjacket. Warm furry bodies pressed against my bare skin, and their companionship is greatly welcomed. Their squeaks are lullabies, and the tiny pink hands seem so human to me, each digit tipped in a perfect claw.

Beady black eyes are my portholes into his movements, and I know that tonight, he means to come. His belly is empty, and he longs for an easy supper. I invited him into the asylum ages ago, so he can come and go as he likes.

The visits are always on his terms, and he has no consideration for convenience.

It doesn't matter anymore. I've heard that lunatics have unnatural strength, so tonight, we'll put that theory to the test.

Inky shadow bleeds through the open window, and it takes form, spanning membranes of wings, broad shoulders, and that long, pale face that I see even in dreams. He grins, and there's nothing in that grin but a reflected hollow.

In nights past, whenever he'd come, I'd feel a mixture of fear and reverence. That's not how I feel on this night.

I feel ready.

*"Open a vein, Renfield. I've come to drink."*

I step forward, looking up at the tall figure that darkens my cell. He is accustomed to being looked up at. He likes for others to feel small; it benefits him.

"You're always thirsty, Count. I've given you every droplet that I have to give, but it's never been enough. You feel entitled to it, don't you? I have something else to give you tonight. A word that you're unaccustomed to hearing."

I step closer to Dracula. The frigid cold of the grave emanates from his form, and when I speak the word that I've saved for him, it comes out nestled in the fog of my breath.

"No."

The brow of porcelain furrows and the ember-eyes burn incredulous in those deep sockets.

*"You'd deny your master? Take that word back and swallow it, Renfield, lest I fold your body into origami and leave you bloodless on the floor."*

He doesn't wait for a response, or even for consent. His long neck snaps downward, and leech lips find their place at the old scars on my throat. Dracula suckles inward, but he quickly releases me, stumbling backward and coughing. He spits a glob of ants and flies out onto the floor.

*"You're empty of plasma. What is this corruption?"*

"Far from empty, Count. As a matter of fact, tonight we've planned a dinner party. I've invited *so* many friends inside."

I smile at Dracula, and bristling spider legs dance behind my teeth.

"Time for you to meet them."

I dart forward, locking arms onto the Count, tightening my grip on him in a firm bearhug. My mouth opens wide, my jaw unhinging in the same method used by constrictor snakes, and pestilence pours forth in an enthusiastic wave. Flies burst out in black clouds, spiders leap and weave their webs in the Count's eyes, rats scurry out from torso, whole legions that nibble at Dracula's softest parts. The centipedes make for his ear canals, the scorpions find his nostrils, and even the ticks turn against him, preying on the predator.

Count Dracula chokes on the vermin, trying in vain to fight the infestation, but it's far too late. Vampires know only how to take, but on this night, the Count learns how to give. He is fed upon against his will, and he rekindles a few shreds of his forgotten humanity, using it to articulate a scream.

I release him, stepping back from the embrace. It will be our last embrace, and for that, I am grateful. He spins in helpless circles, clawing at himself, rending that dead pallid flesh into ribbons, but he gets no closer to exorcising the little demons that have entered him from groin to gullet.

When it's over, he is just a cloak and cinders piled onto the floor. The insects paint themselves in his ashes.

I kneel onto my scabbed knees one last time, for nostalgia's sake, and I blow with everything within me.

I scatter him across the floor of the cell, and come morning, he'll be swept up.

The open window awaits, and with skittering legs, translucent wings, and questing claws, we go.

---

**Jeremy Megargee** has always loved dark fiction. He cut his teeth on R.L Stine's *Goosebumps* series as a child and a fascination with Stephen King, Jack London, Algernon Blackwood, and many others followed later in life. Jeremy weaves his tales of personal horror from Martinsburg, West Virginia with his cat Lazarus acting as his muse/familiar. He is a member of the West Virginia chapter of the Horror Writer's Association and you can often find him peddling his dark words in various mountain hollers deep within the Appalachians.

# The Killing Jar
## By Mark Oxbrow

Tell no one. My college motto was '*Quod tacitum velis nemini dixeris.*' 'That which you wish to be secret, tell to nobody.'

But here I sit and write, telling you all my secrets and praying that you will forgive me.

You beseech me to tell you everything. Keep nothing secret. No matter how unwise that seems, I will do all I can.

Apologies for my ungodly handwriting. Half of a bottle of 25-Year-Old Single Malt appears to have vanished since midnight. Do you remember drinking Islay Whisky Sours in the Palm Room at the Tivoli? And you singing 'The Maid's Conjuring Book'?

Your brother drunk and laughing, throwing sugar cubes at the maître d'.

I met your brother at Oxford. He took Law at Magdalen. I was at Trinity College studying nothing of consequence. I believe he told you that we met in the quadrangle and that I was lost and close to tears. That was untrue. I was in fact climbing an oak tree in Wytham Woods.

'What the devil are you doing?' he shouted up at me.

'Collecting.' I replied. '*Satyrium pruni.*'

'What on Earth?'

'*Satyrium pruni.* The Black Hairstreak. It's quite rare.'

The woods provide sanctuary to hundreds of species of butterflies and moths. Like a fool, I was clambering out on a bough with my butterfly net and collecting tools. I remember your brother was fascinated by the killing jar. I made it with a glass jar and a small amount of cyanide of potassium. The butterfly would dance and flutter for no more than a few seconds.

It was his eyes I noticed first. The most piercing blue, but irregular, one pupil large and black. Like a music hall mesmerist.

Thick as thieves. That's what they said of us. Forty years ago. Hobnell and Renfield. We never did use our Christian names. Hobnell and Renfield, like we were some arcane firm of dusty accountants.

Renfield was diligent where I was neglectful, immaculate as I was disheveled. He would write the labels for my butterflies. Tiny copperplate letters on minute slivers of paper. *Aglais urticae*, the small tortoiseshell. *Pararge aegeria*, the speckled wood butterfly.

I would inspect the fallen trees as they rotted into the ground. I picked grubs and beetles from the deadwood. And Renfield was my willing accomplice.

It was inevitable that your brother would excel. We toasted his success at the Eagle and Child and my failure at the Lamb and Flag! I don't think my father ever forgave me for abandoning politics for science. Of all the lamentable things I have done and left undone, I never regretted this decision. I devoted myself entirely to entomology.

Renfield's Bloomsbury house was barely a half mile as the crow flies from my work at the British Museum. I'm afraid that you have me to blame for the Morris 'Acanthus' wallpaper. The place was ghastly when he bought it and he gave me carte blanche to decorate from the drapes to the doorbell.

The Windham Club, in the northwest corner of St. James's Square, became his second home. Your brother kindly paid my entrance fee, as £26 and 5 shillings was beyond my means at the time.

I vividly recall Renfield at the Inner Temple. His law chambers were little more than a hovel. I could have mistaken him for an alchemist or a necromancer in his black robes. He never did suit the wig. He seemed perpetually ill at ease, like something was crawling under his skin. His smile was lost somewhere in those heaps of legal papers. I never saw him so miserable.

That was the first time he vanished.

I grew accustomed to his disappearances in later years but to go without a word of explanation seemed bizarrely out of character then. Three months. Nothing but a telegram from Edinburgh. 'Needn't worry. Back September. Stop.'

He refused to say where he had been or what business he had in Scotland. His law career ended abruptly and ingloriously. He insisted I help him burn his papers and law books on a bonfire in Bloomsbury Square. He threw his wig and wig stand into the flames and he smiled. I'd never been so glad to see him smile.

Do you recall when he first introduced us? It was in Brighton. Your mother had sent you away to the Brighton Female Convalescent Home to get you out of London and 'far away from temptation.' I never forgot the first thing you ever said to me.

You leaned close, whispering in my ear:

'I have been banished for debauching a governess!'

I think your mother was under the delusion that you and I might marry. She certainly hoped that a regime of walks on stone beaches, salt air and standing knee-deep in the sea might cure you, a daughter of Sappho!

You were a revelation. Delightful. A being of pure joy. I saw your brother so clearly, lit by your light. I saw the burden he carried fall away. Saw a glimmer of the children you once were. Chasing seagulls. Throwing rocks into the sea.

We abducted you from your sanatorium and took a day trip to Bramber. Of all the things to recall so vividly I can still picture the bizarre exhibits of Mr. Potter's Museum of Curiosities. I was used to seeing lifelike wonders stuffed and stitched by some of the finest taxidermists in the Empire. But here was a carnival of grotesques. Squirrels and rabbits, birds and kittens. Misshapen, handsewn and posed. I could not decide if Mr. Potter was genius or madman.

You laughed and babbled, squinting at each ridiculous creation. Renfield was transfixed, lost for words.

Cock Robin, dead in his tiny coffin, carried to his grave by feathered pallbearers. Squirrels smoking cigars. Dead eyed rabbits, in school, scrawling on slates. Kittens playing at croquet. Kittens taking tea from miniature teapots. And a kitten in her wedding dress. White lace and silk. Glass eyes. Her veil stitched to her fur.

'Mister Potter,' your brother said reverently, 'The kittens… tell me, did you drown the kittens?'

I saw it that day. A thing I'd put out of my mind. The look in Renfield's eyes as he stared at the butterflies in the killing jar.

We haunted London's most reputable taxidermists that winter. Found exotic birds and curious beasts for the house in Bloomsbury. Owls and osprey. The baboon. And our mongoose, fangs bared, fighting that cobra, tooth and claw. My musty cases of pinned and labelled butterflies seemed dull in contrast, but Renfield insisted they should hang from every picture rail.

It must have been odd for you to be out from under your mother's relentless gaze. Settled in your brother's house and let loose. We three stayed out till dawn, sleeping through the days, the curtains drawn. Inseparable and unleashed. Renfield put so much Jamaica rum in the eggnog that Christmas that I barely survived the parson's sermon.

That January he disappeared.

You wanted to fetch the police. To scour the banks of the Thames for his body. You were so convinced of his demise. Dead in a snowfield you said. February came and went. Then March brought a letter from Rome with vague apologies and 'do not fear.' April saw Renfield back on the doorstep. All smiles and secrets. Whatever he was doing, it paid well enough. Far better than the law had ever done.

When I pressed Renfield on the matter all he ever said was he was working 'for the good of Queen and Country.'

I spied him once in the Windham Club taking luncheon with the Prince of Wales and the Duke of Cambridge. He saw me, called me over and introduced me as if there was nothing peculiar about the company he kept. We drank wine and talked about wives, actresses and mistresses. Bertie breathed a scandalous story about Lillie Langtry. The Duke roared, recalling his wife's high jinks backstage at Covent Garden Theatre, Drury Lane and the Lyceum.

The closest I ever got to uncovering Renfield's secrets was in Paris. Your brother and I found lodgings in Montmartre a fortnight before you joined us. We haunted the cabarets, cafés, and bars. The Moulin de la Galette and the Chat Noir.

One evening Renfield took me with him to meet a gaunt fierce man he called Aleksei. The two sat close and spoke in what I can only imagine was Russian. I have read that émigrés fleeing the Tsar found refuge in Paris. Anarchists and dissidents. It took Aleksei an hour of drinking to find a smile. At midnight, Renfield led us through a labyrinth of narrow streets to a brothel. The madame knew your brother, kissing his face, repeating his name.

Renfield confessed, before you sailed from England, that he wished I would propose to you. What an odd family we would have made. The spinster and the bachelor.

The night you arrived we shared a bottle of absinthe. Renfield dripped laudanum into our glasses from a small vial and lit our drinks with a long match. Sugar and silver spoons and the green fairy. Like a magical elixir.

Renfield wanted to be out. In a brasserie or a bawdyhouse. You wanted to take a bath and I wanted nothing but sleep. Renfield left his book that night. *A Study in Scarlet*. He'd always kept it close at hand. I found a scrap of paper between the pages. The writing on the paper said: 'Peter Ivanovich Rachkovsky'. And, inked in the same minute copperplate he reserved for my butterfly labels, were a series of small numbers. I put the paper back in place and never spoke if it to your brother.

The end came fast. Out of nowhere. Without mercy or an ounce of pity.

That summer you had made the acquaintance of Ada Nettleship, a most remarkable seamstress. If I recall, you were besotted with her. Ada was to sew a dress for a production at the Lyceum Theatre and in a bid to win her affection you promised to find her a thousand jewel beetle wings. Ada's suppliers had come up wanting and it seemed that knowing an entomologist might finally be of use.

Oddly it was not my colleagues and peers at the Entomological Society of London that provided the aid we so desperately needed. It was a Brother Mason, a solicitor by the name of Hawkins from Devonshire.

Brother Hawkins was a fine stout fellow. As far from our Bohemian ways as it is possible to imagine. We met by chance at the Windham Club. Renfield and I slouched in the library, comparing notes and lamenting our lack of beetle wings.

'Excuse me, gentlemen.'

A small voice interrupted our conversation.

'I'm afraid that I could not help overhearing. You require a quantity of jewel beetle wings?'

Brother Hawkins introduced himself properly: Mister Peter Hawkins, solicitor, of Exeter.

Hawkins had travelled to London to view a particular property for a distant client. At that moment a mutual friend arrived, Percival Wickham of the Ordnance Store Corps. Wickham is, as they say, an acquired taste. Renfield and I knew him from the Jerusalem Lodge, one of London's Red Apron Freemasonic Lodges. Peter Hawkins met Wickham at the Lodge of the Nine Muses.

Wickham was to introduce Hawkins to the owner of Carfax Abbey and Estate. He knew the man well as his military career saw him command the Royal Gunpowder Magazine at Purfleet. God alone knows why anyone would put a fellow like Wickham in charge of enough gunpowder to destroy half of Essex.

The four of us shared a bottle of port and discussed iridescent beetle wings and the Carpathian Mountains. Hawkins had sold a modest property near the Tobacco Dock to the infamous Charles Jamrach of Jamrach's Animal Emporium on Ratcliffe Highway. Mr. Jamrach imports exotic animals and birds from every continent. I recalled reading in *The Times* that Charles Jamrach had sold a Norwegian grey wolf named 'Berserker' to the London Zoological Gardens.

Peter Hawkins was sure that Jamrach would stock the jewel beetle wings that we desired.

As the evening wore on Hawkins told us, in confidence, that he was to inspect the property in Purfleet for a mysterious aristocratic client. As well as the Abbey and Estate in Purfleet, the gentleman intended to buy properties across the city. Hawkins had never met him in the flesh. He was a recluse, a nobleman that lived in his ancestral castle, deep in the Carpathian Mountains.

'The Carpathians?' Renfield spluttered into his glass. 'Transylvania?'

Renfield spoke of crossing the Carpathian Mountains, travelling from Budapest to Varna. Murky forests and yawning chasms. Villages that seemed to grow out of the rocks. Hawkins wondered aloud if Renfield ever intended to return. To my surprise, Renfield revealed that he planned a trip to Constantinople, Bucharest, and Odessa before the end of the year.

Peter Hawkins's advice was invaluable.

Jamrach's Emporium was intoxicating. An incredible menagerie of beast and birds. Cages heaped like hatboxes. Floor after floor of wonders. A black jaguar paced in its den. Llamas from South America, Monkeys, tapir, boa, porcupines, black swans, and gazelle. A fox from the Arctic Circle and two ferocious tigers from India.

Among the snarling beasts and screeching birds, Jamrach had cabinets of marine shells from distant islands, narwhal horns, and boxes of shimmering jewel beetle wings. And we found something more. A present for you. Three tiny white mice. Rescued from certain death as a python's dinner.

We returned in triumph with our prize. Conquering heroes. And you fell quite in love with your tiny white mice. They scurried about in your hair, snuffling at your ears as you giggled. You would hide them in your evening bag and feed them scraps from the table. The Three Graces you called them: Euphrosyne, Aglaia, Thalia.

Ada Nettleship was elated. Boxes of beautiful blue-green beetle wings. She press-ganged you, Renfield and I into her bevy of seamstresses. The premiere of Macbeth at the Lyceum was barely two nights away. We stitched by gaslight, sewing hundreds of damned beetle wings onto Lady Macbeth's emerald dress.

I confess to failure at needlecraft. I may be adept at pinning a butterfly without damaging its fragile wings, but needles are not pins. 'Who would have thought the old man to have had so much blood in him?' Shakespeare's words were never more appropriate.

That night at the Lyceum was astonishing. Henry Irving stalked the stage, dagger in hand. And Ellen Terry. Gods, the moment she appeared. Lady Macbeth. Dressed in emerald green and velvet cloak. A thousand jeweled wings caught the limelight and the theatre gasped and held its breath.

And you left for Venice that Monday. Venice, Florence, then to Paris with your new love. Renfield was to leave that Wednesday. Off to Constantinople and parts unknown, and in his suitcase a parcel of legal documents from Mr. Peter Hawkins. Renfield would meet Hawkins's client, a Count Dracula, in the Carpathians. We were to meet for luncheon in the Windham on the first of the month.

Renfield never made it to the Windham.

I fed your mice. A month passed. Then two. I visited the house in Bloomsbury. A vase was smashed near the stairs. There was a painting askew. A streak of blood on the banister. *A Study in Scarlet* lay torn to pieces but Renfield was nowhere to be found.

My telegram brought you back to London. That evening I came to visit you, hoping you may have heard something. I heard your screams as I unlocked the front door.

Renfield was in the library. You were huddled in the corner, rocking, cradling your knees in your arms. Oak bookcases lay toppled, books torn apart, pages trampled underfoot. Renfield had smashed the lamps. He paced the room, muttering and babbling. I saw that he had broken the butterfly cases. Splintered glass littered the floor. Renfield had pulled the pins out one by one. Taken every specimen from its frame. And eaten it.

He raised a moth up before his face, sliding it between his lips.

'Renfield?' I whispered his name.

His head darted around. He tilted it to one side, staring at me. He had no inkling who I was.

There was something in his hand. I couldn't make it out.

'Blood.' Renfield said.

I glanced across at you. Saw your dress cut open, blood spattered across your face.

Renfield gnawed at his fingers. He had bandaged them with thin strips of rag, ripped from his shirt sleeve. Nails torn to the quick. Flesh bitten from bone.

'Blood.'

I saw you shudder.

'Look,' Renfield shuffled to the writing bureau.

There was a straight razor in his hand.

'Made them.' Renfield sniffed.

He wiped his nose with the back of his hand.

'Made them for you.'

He picked up a small bundle, raising his hands to show us.

'Pretty brides.'

I saw them then.

And a scream strangled in my throat. Ice in my blood.

'Pretty.'

Your three white mice. Renfield had made them wedding dresses. Torn pieces of silk and cotton. Hand stitched and sewn in neat little lines. Three brides. Their heads sliced off. My butterfly pins jagged through their fur.

Renfield licked at the blood on his razor.

You fought to stand, steadying yourself against a bookshelf, and your brother shrieked and threw himself at you.

Hands clawed. The razor slashed your thigh. I saw you fumble at your hair as I leapt across the room. You pulled a jeweled hatpin from your hair and stabbed at Renfield. Six inches of silver stuck through his face.

The razor dropped from Renfield's hand as you snatched the hatpin out of his cheek, stabbing at his neck. He stumbled back, shrieking. And you jammed the silver hatpin an inch above his eye.

I found a private asylum beside the Carfax Estate in Purfleet. Wickham vouched for the doctor that had bought the property. Doctor Jack Seward. He seemed awfully young to be a doctor, but he appeared to be a capable alienist. He committed himself to discovering the cause of your brother's lunacy.

I found it near impossible to visit Renfield in that place. How could the man I knew be so corrupted? Seward quickly ruled out syphilis. By some miracle your brother had avoided the pox with bangtails from Seven Dials to Le Chabanais. It was so unnatural to see Renfield in the asylum. He seemed so small, so helpless. Caged liked some animal in Jamrach's menagerie.

'Master?' Renfield mumbled.

God knows who he thought I was.

He ate grubs and flies. Picked at them in the dirt and fed them to a grotesque bloated spider.

'Life. You see?' he looked to the ceiling as if he might be overheard.

I could not bear it. How could Renfield become so degraded? What thing had broken his mind?

Dr Seward pressed Renfield ceaselessly, seeking to define and diagnose his affliction. Seward classified Renfield as a zoöphagous, an eater of life. Classified. Latin or Greek. Like an insect. Zoöphagous. Labeled neatly on a sliver of paper.

'Blood.' I barely heard his words.

'What?'

'Blood.' Renfield repeated. 'The blood is the life.'

I couldn't tell you the things he said. I feared what it would do to you. I was a fool to think you were so fragile, but I wanted to protect you. I am sorry for that. The truth may have hurt you less.

Your treatment at Wood End Private Asylum stands in stark contrast to Renfield's in Purfleet. There is a lock on your door, but your room is comfortable and brightly lit. Bouquets of cut flowers sit in vases in the corridors. You are given canvas and easel and encouraged to paint. There are gardens to walk, bees and butterflies, and peace to be found.

It is midwinter night. Maybe by spring I will hand you this letter and tell you the truth. By then I hope you will be healed. I will take you back to Paris. Help you pick up the threads of your life. I will tell you that your brother is dead. His life was taken during the night of 3 October. It was quick. At the end he regained some sense of himself that I thought lost forever.

I know you will want to bury Renfield's remains in your family crypt. I am sorry for what I have to tell you, but I dare not regret what I have done. Professor Abraham Van Helsing made me swear you see. Swear on all that is Holy. He feared that your brother might return from out his grave. Feared the contagion that took his life.

Dr Seward's attendants stitched Renfield into a linen shroud and he was buried at the edge of consecrated ground. I was the only mourner at his graveside. The following Monday, a police inspector paid me a visit. Renfield's grave had been violated he said. An outrage had been committed. I thanked the officer for his consideration. He thought it curious that I did not ask the nature of the violation. I simply said I did not want to know.

But I had no need to ask.

I dug your brother out of his grave. Dragged his corpse to a scrap of woodland and cut him from his shroud. Renfield. There was no hint of corruption. No blood at his mouth. I sat with him, under an oak tree. I touched his face. The man I loved.

I took the shovel and hacked his head from his body. I heaped deadwood and leaves on his corpse and burned it.

But I had nothing of his. No memento to cherish. I had to do it you see. So I took his eyes and placed his head upon the pyre.

I keep them still. Collected in the killing jar.

**Mark Oxbrow** is a storyteller, author and ghost writer. His short story, 'No Doves Come from Raven's Eggs,' was recommended by legendary editor, Ellen Datlow, as one of the best horror short stories of the year in 2019. Truant Pictures (an Animal Logic company) shortlisted Mark's horror screenplay 'She Awakens' for their inaugural genre screenplay competition. Mark's books feature ghost stories, witch goddesses, Arthurian legends, poison gardens, folk horror, medieval monsters and secret treasures. Over twenty years ago, Mark founded the largest Halloween festival in Scotland.

# Life Eater
## By Kelli Owen

My heart skipped a beat as I watched the man slice the filthy woman's throat. The overwhelming waft of her drunkenness mixed with the sudden release of urine in the night air. He moved like the shadows, as at ease in the darkened backyard as a tomcat out for a pre-dawn stroll. *Nothing* extraordinary stood out about him — average height and weight, simple clothing, a fashionable hairstyle and neatly kept facial hair. You could pass him several times over and not remember seeing him, and yet he was the embodiment of passion, power, and something deeper. Something more feral than the tomcat he mimicked, more raw than the death he left in his wake.

He was, in a word, *magical.*

Not as commanding a presence as my last master, he was nonetheless brimming with raw talent. Though his work was, shall we say, *sophomoric*, and could be improved upon with the right motivation. Finding myself with both the time and knowledge, I was eager to help him reach his full potential.

He *needed* me.

I watched with wide eyes, the hand over my mouth *barely* hiding my growing smile, as he lowered himself to the now still body in the quiet backyard. Lifting her skirts and exposing her decency, he jabbed the glimmering steel into her pubis and pushed the blade away from him with a single forceful thrust, opening her torso in a jagged line of hurried excitement. Reaching in, he pulled at the viscera, slicing it free before extracting it to drape over her shoulder. He turned his attention back toward the cavity he'd created, the blood-slicked ropes of pale intestines discarded, or displayed, glistening in the moonlight. I gasped at the raw beauty of it all and he turned toward the sound.

Our eyes met as I pushed my back against the wall, my shoulders drooping in a subservient posture. He was the artist, and I but the audience. He stood, eyes narrowing as his grip on the knife tightened. A heavy exhale created a plume of breath in the cold morning air, and his countenance shifted. He pivoted on a heel and came toward me. I accepted my fate and lowered my eyes. Instead, I heard the soft crunching of his boots on the loose gravel of the alleyway move *away* from me. I looked up and watched as he slipped into the dark shadows beyond the meager streetlights.

I approached the body and thought back to my Carpathian master and his untimely demise. Not one to waste such blissful nourishment, he would not have spilled a single drop of blood. I felt less sorrow at his passing than of the unfulfilled promises which followed him to the grave. Many presumed I had also perished. I thought it best to let them believe so and made my way from Carfax Abbey to hide in the less desirable portion of London's East End.

I looked down at the woman sprawled below me and smiled. My insomnia-induced wanderings of the neighborhood had proven fortuitous. I would not have otherwise stumbled upon the man. I wouldn't have the pangs of excitement at the prospect of a new master.

Squatting beside the body, I studied the exposed organs and licked my lips. Flies and spiders and birds had barely enough blood to taste a sampling of life, but *this?* The beautiful organ left for me was not a mere *sampling* of life but the very house in which it was created. Reaching inside, eager to feel its still warm vitality, I pulled the womb toward me, two flicks of my penknife freeing it from captivity. The clock tower at the Black Eagle Brewery chimed, and I stood as if I had been struck. Holding my prize tight, I scurried down Brick Lane toward my dosshouse on Flower and Dean Street.

**M**y day off was spent in a delirium of senses. Slipping into my room as a mouse moved through a busy kitchen, I avoided the other tenants. I set my prize into the shallow basin bowl on my dresser and stared at it for quite some time, half expecting it to tell me its secrets.

I finally blinked away the idea of its consciousness and thought of Dr. Seward and his claims of my *illness*. I had scoffed then and mocked him still — for those who do not understand brilliance often go to task labeling such as *conditions*. He had called me a *life eater*, though he'd used a fancy term with Latin roots when he spoke to others. My nibbling on insects and small creatures was mistaken as a craving for *blood*, but was instead the search for the spark of life itself. Now I had life in my basin bowl, its fluids smearing the white porcelain, its rich coppery tang filling my nose.

And I knew just what to do with it.

The first small piece I tasted was raw, and while the flavor itself was neither unexpected nor unappetizing, the texture was mildly sinewy. I took the time to slowly cook the next piece over the flame of several candles bound together to increase their heat. The texture was improved, but the taste had changed, leaning toward the rich organ meats one often found in stuffing or sweetbread. Its origin masked, its power became subjectively diminished.

After cutting several small bits and placing them in an old lard jar I had been scraping for my bread — saving them for future nibbles — I opened the remaining portion with a single thin slice along its grain. Laying it out like butterfly wings, I took a deep breath, the heady aroma drifting up at me anew and forcing my eyes closed in a moment of pleasure. While the meat had grown cold, the blood inside had been protected and now leaked free in a slow dribble of gravity to pool under the carnage. I poured what remained of yesterday's water pitcher into the bowl and grabbed the sponge.

*Did the whispers of Bathory's sins have merit?*

I slowly stripped off my garments and stood naked before the bowl, my flesh humming with electrical anticipation. I spent the next hour wiping down my body with the tainted water, occasionally licking it from my fingers. When I was spent and could take no more, I collapsed onto my bed sheets and fell into a deep satisfying sleep.

When I awoke, I knew I needed to find the man. I craved more, but didn't have the heart for the act itself. I was compelled to locate the artist who had introduced me to possibilities my previous master had held back from me. I would shadow his genius, praying at the font of his victims.

I spent the better part of a fortnight scouring the streets. While not alone in that endeavor, I — unlike the police — knew who I was looking for. They carried on about Dark Annie and Polly, asking their questions and deducing from clumsy crime scenes and confused witnesses. I hunted the shadows of taverns and alleys for the face I'd never forget. I searched during the wee hours when I should have been sleeping, accepting my insomnia and choosing to catch my respite after my shift with Henry Smith, the Hanbury Street undertaker.

The first several days after the murder proved quite exciting, as the body whose organ I had tasted sat in stasis at my very worksite, her burial stalled by investigators. The following Friday, officials finally took her body away, to be laid to rest at Manor Park Cemetery. Upon leaving work, I nearly tripped over the man, busy as I was, daydreaming and paying no mind to my route. I had turned to cross the street and stumbled into a figure bent low, adjusting the laces of his boots.

"Good pardon, Sir." I spoke my apology and backed up, shame painted on my face.

"Indeed." He stood and walked away, giving me no cursory glance of forgiveness.

But I had seen his face — if only for a flash, if only from the side — and I recognized it immediately. In elation, my hand shot out to tap his shoulder but I pulled it back, a frightened child reaching for affection it had not yet earned. I composed myself and waited while he crossed the street and continued down the cobblestones.

A beat later, I followed.

We passed Flower and Dean Street, and I glanced at my rented door. Seemingly unaware of me in tow, he crossed Whitechapel Road and followed Commercial for but a minute before he turned onto Batty. The small, dark street was little more than a glorified alley. Its shadows were caused by tall, over-crowded dosshouses along both sides with a smattering of private rooms in view.

The man was not paying a tuppence for standing room or sixpence for shared quarters. He stopped at a painted door, which meant he enjoyed the luxury of a private room, and at this, I smiled. Likely as small as my own, but it would be enough to offer the man somewhere to clean up and unwind, to relive the things he'd done during the night. Privately.

I looked back the way we'd traveled and thought of the route. It was but a handful of blocks from the murder scene — a straight shot on even the darkest night. With enough building alcoves to tuck into and alley shadows to slip among, I could easily imagine how he'd gotten home without suspicion or arrest.

Not only had I found him on this glorious day, I knew where he lived.

The following weeks were a blur of anxiety and enthusiasm. I followed him nightly, as often and for as long as I could afford. I didn't question his authority or knowledge, but did wonder how he felt about the papers claiming he'd taken her womb.

*Did he know it had been my doing? Did it intrigue him? Did he approve?*

I slipped carefully crafted letters under his door, offering him sanction and praise, and leaving suggestions for further concepts. On one occasion, I included an anatomical illustration I'd torn from a book and marked up with notes, showing him which organs would garner the most reward. I underlined the uterus several times in hopes he would understand.

The police and press were also busy throughout September. One with nothing for leads, forced to double patrols on the streets and ask the same questions of the same people, over and again. The other falsified evidence for the sake of their morning edition, as an industrious journalist crafted a persona for the man, complete with a motive and moniker. I shook my head at the intense disrespect, as the man was suddenly given a title to be whispered among the fallen women and their drunken cohorts.

I must admit, when I first read the *Dear Boss* letter in the paper, I immediately thought back to Dr. Seward at the sanitarium, first name John, though often called Jack. But he was neither the fictitious creation, nor the man himself. Whoever had written the letter had succeeded in exactly one thing, an illustrious endeavor, which led police further away from the truth.

T hree days after the letter was printed in the papers, the man went out after midnight. He *slammed* his door shut, which made me question his motives then, and to this day. Was he itching to create art, or simply lashing out at the articles and false claims about him?

I followed him in and out of alleys. I waited while he stopped at each pub, pausing long enough for a drink in Ten Bells, but otherwise seeming to be popping in and out, as if seeking someone. We had traveled up and down The East End and were almost back to the man's house when a woman's voice called from the shadows of the gateway for Dutfield's Yard, "Want the business?"

I had spent weeks watching the man, and had seen the women who come and go this time of night. The fallen women. Those put out on the streets. Even with menial work, they never seemed to have the funds needed to secure a bed for the night without trolloping about the streets and actively choosing *not* to spend whatever tuppence they made on liquor. I could tell by her clothing and filth, and the pre-death stench that wafted from her, this was one such woman. And I instantly realized what the man must have surely already known — she wouldn't be missed.

He nodded at her and stepped toward the gate, presumably intent to slip into the darkness beyond to take care of her in ways she had not considered.

*Finally*, I thought. *More life.*

Another man suddenly appeared in front of me, having crossed the street to my side to avoid the couple at the gateway. Had he seen the master's face? Could he identify him?

I took a step toward the stranger and he baulked at my presence, picking up his speed and hurrying away. Any concern I may have had for the situation was well under consideration by the man, as I looked back to the gateway and watched him reach out, the gleaming edge in his hand swiping with quick, angry precision. The woman fell to the ground. The man looked down the street in the direction the stranger had gone, and quickly turned to go the opposite way. The opportunity ruined, the scene contaminated.

I hastened to follow him.

Keeping my distance, so as not to startle what may have been the man's already frayed nerves, I shadowed him west as he weaved in and out of streets and alleys, no longer seeming interested in pubs or groups of people. At the corner of Duke and Church Passage, he stopped. I almost didn't see the woman standing there, but upon hearing her standard proffer of cunny for coin, there was no mistaking the slur in her voice. The man led her up the alley to Mitre Square.

As I watched — the warmth blossoming in my chest like it had the first time — he brought the knife out and slashed across her throat, the moonlight glinting off the blade. Working quickly, the man again ripped open the abdomen and pulled the intestines free. Though rather than digging further into the cavity, he paused and studied her a moment, before striking at her face violently with the knife tip in one hand and the fist of his other. He hacked blindly, cutting a piece off her ear. The seething rage on his face made me wonder what exactly had gotten into him, and I looked around, frightful someone would notice the commotion.

Returning to her abdomen, he dug around with both hands, tearing bits free to set on the ground next to her. Finally liberating the prize he sought, he held the organ with both hands and stopped all motion. He looked around furtively and stood quickly, as if he'd heard something I had not. He turned in my direction as I stepped from the shadows. I nodded to him. Solemnly. He scowled and scurried off in the other direction.

*Did he not recognize me?*

I approached the body to review his work, to revel in the beauty of his art, but what I found disturbed me. Yes, he had indeed taken her life for his own passions and rummaged through her innards to find the parts he treasured, but he had mutilated her without cause. There was nothing graceful about what he'd done to her face, or the clear destruction of her core.

*Had he known her?*

*Did she remind him of someone?*

There had to be a reason for such disregard of the magic behind murder.

I bent down to closer examine the open wound and remnants left behind, only to shake my head at the sight. The man had gone too high, reaching under her ribs, and had removed her kidney rather than her uterus. The beautiful purple life-giving organ sat intact, glistening, as if welcoming me to take it. I needed no gilded invitation, and retrieved my penknife.

As I slipped back into the shadows, hurrying to catch up, I was eager to see what the man would do with his chosen organ. As I followed him, I thought of the difference between this body and the first. The escalation of rage. The lack of decorum. Taking life and enjoying the flesh which holds it is one thing, but utterly destroying the face and form which had contained it? There was something not right. Where the man had raw talent and the taste for blood, he had no elegance.

I was disappointed for a second time that night at his decision to dispose of the bounty he'd taken. Discarded as if it were no longer a treasure, a prize.

I began to question whether he was truly a worthy master.


**I**t took me almost a week to enjoy every last bit of tissue and blood from the womb. I hated being away from it while at work, and would rush home to relish the bloody water or enjoy nibbles from my lard jar. In that time, the police had grown more baffled, almost angry at their incompetence, while the newspapers and rags were getting bolder — printing more and more lies and *supposed* correspondence from the man.

What they called the *Letter From Hell* was intrinsically preposterous, but being accompanied by half a kidney was *proof* it hadn't come from the man. I had followed him home that night and had seem him toss his trophy over a fence to quiet a barking dog. I had also learned in that moment, the man's art was not in partaking in the aftermath such as I did, but rather in creating chaos in the first place. The memory of flavor flicked through my mind as I licked my lips and silently thanked him for leaving me the best part.

For all of October, I followed him fruitlessly. He came and went as if he were a *normal* man. As if he had no underlying gifts making his bland visage a disguise of ordinary. I began to worry I had spooked him.

*Was my being there twice too much for him? Did he believe I was police?*

I grew bold out of necessity, pushing my boundaries and stretching the limits of safety. I made a point of purposely crossing his path during daylight hours and tipping my hat, a silent nod of respect and recognition. I slipped another letter under his door, assuring him I meant no harm and only wished to bathe in the beauty of his artistry.

*Did my talk of grace and hopes for improved panache worry him?*

*Was he afraid he couldn't live up to my expectations?*

I feared my boldness in the situation had flipped the power dynamic and he was now waiting for *me* to act. I stood in the stoop across from his as the rain slowed to a drizzle, fully expecting him to stay in due to the weather. I was about to go home and pen a lengthy discourse, explaining my desires for his success, but lo, he stepped from his house with a familiar stride. I could see his expression clearly in the meager streetlight. The wicked twist of a smile slid across his face as he glanced about.

*Looking for me?*

He stepped from his stoop with confidence. He was back. He was on the prowl, and I in silent pursuit.

Unlike so many other nights, the man didn't meander in and out of streets and alleys, or bother going in and out of the handful of pubs dotting The East End. He seemed to make a beeline for none other than my own neighborhood.

At first, I was certain he'd discovered exactly who I was and where I was boarding. I feared he may perceive me as a threat to his anonymity or person, and that he was intent on ending me. My brows furrowed with worry as we approached Flower and Dean and turned to head down it.

Without so much as a glance at my door, the man went straight through to the other end of the block and turned north on Leman Street. Upon approach, he promptly walked into the Ten Bells pub and left me standing on the street, wondering if I had mistaken his confidence and return to grace as something else. I slouched against the still wet brick wall and listened to the distant clock of Black Eagle Brewery as it chimed half past three.

In less than a quarter hour, the man emerged from the pub, the foam of the pint he'd enjoyed still clinging to his mustache. He wiped his cuff across his face and set out with a determined step. Barely crossing the street, he'd drawn the attention of someone looking to make his acquaintance.

The dollymop looked him up and down and whistled sweetly. She was younger than the women the man had previously approached, and far prettier. With a wink and a nod she offered, "Roll for a tuppence?"

The man nodded and followed her down the darkness of Dorset Street toward the dimly lit courtyard at the back. I slowed my gait, expecting them to stop at any moment — where she would expect him to push her against the wall for a three-penny-upright, but where he would surprise her with an opened throat and quick death.

Neither of these things happened.

He followed her to the end of the dark alleyway and stopped in front of a door. The sound of her fumbling for a key was ice in my veins.

*What is he doing?*

*He cannot go inside. He cannot be part of her life, only her death. He cannot…*

My thought trailed off as it jumbled with many others in a mental cacophony of panic and uncertainty. The man had broken rule number one — never, *ever*, return to their home. I saw my previous master do so, and fall because of it. It gives the victim the upper hand. It offers too many chances for mistakes. It provides an environment for evidence to be left behind.

My eyes swam with hot tears of dread, my breath quickened.

I hurried to the door, intent on stepping in, *interrupting*, doing whatever I could to stop this from happening. Alas, the door closed before I reached it, the poignant sound of the lock clicking into place. With trepidation, I slipped around the corner in hopes of finding egress. A window offered me a view I had not expected.

The young girl had already removed her dress, and it was neatly folded on the chair. The man was also naked, his clothing set on the floor near the door.

*Is this actually nothing more than amorous congress?*

*No.*

I realized my folly when I watched the man turn to away from me to face her, the knife gripped in a fist behind him. I held my breath as he approached her. In slow motion he brought his hand forward. He reached for her with his free hand as he allowed her to see the weapon. Her eyes widened, her mouth opened, but before the scream escaped, the blade moved through air and flesh and bone. Her expression and the burbling blood at the wound made me believe I could hear the sounds of her death through the pane of glass between us. I leaned closer and grasped my chest as he laid her back on the bed and continued to work.

Whether he finally believed himself to be an artist or not, the man made quick work of her body. But something was different. The animalistic brutality of his postmortem attacks was almost overbearing, and I looked away more than once.

The man didn't simply cut the young woman open. Rather, the night flower's petals were plucked as he peeled the flesh from her thighs and stomach, pulling and slicing, freeing a bit at a time, as if skinning a fish. He discarded the flaps and shifted his attention to her bosom. With several strokes of his blade, he removed both of the girl's breasts. I barely had time to swallow back the bile threatening my throat, before he moved to her core, opening her center and pulling free all within reach.

The man placed her organs around the body, almost as if to display them to the gods, or the police.

*Is he staging the scene for the press photographer?*

He dropped the intestines to the side of the body and dug below them. A small lump of bloodied tissue was placed on the other side. He stopped, raised his knife, and spoke to her, his words unclear but his tone chastising, his grimace a leering triumph.

He slashed at her arms and legs. He stabbed at the angry wounds where her breasts had been. He frenzied about her face, the wake of his attack cleaving her nose free, gouging her eyes, shredding her lips, and all but severing her ear from her scalp.

The man withdrew the kidney and placed it with one breast beneath her head, a strange pillow of which only he understood the design. The remnants of her other breast were cast against the wall to bounce back and land near her right foot. Her liver was retrieved and set between her feet.

Blood splashed his arena of rage. It seeped and pooled onto the dance floor of his macabre. The mattress was dark with fluids. The floor was slick from her weeping arteries. The gore covered him, and I understood why he'd removed his clothing. *He'd known what he wanted to do.*

The man grinned, his teeth a pearly beacon amidst his blood smeared face. He grabbed the knife and cut the uterus free, holding it in front of him reverently for a moment, before putting it under her head with the other organs. I blanched, as he resumed the blade and blunt-fisted attacks on her, finding an enemy among her pubis and buttocks, leaving the ruddy pre-bruise marks and opening her flesh in dozens of yawning wounds. His expression twisted from anger to pleasure and back again, as he brought his knife down over and over, wildly attacking whatever flesh remained unmarked.

Finally he sat back and silently assessed what he'd done.

I felt sick. Spent. I had watched a madman unleash hell for no reason other than destruction. In what had felt like hours but had taken less than half of one, her life-giving organs had been completely destroyed. *All* of her had been destroyed. She was no longer recognizable as the young girl I'd seen a short time before.

This was not art.

This man was no artist.

This was the work of a maniac. A monster. A beast fueled by rage and hate rather than beauty and grace.

I swallowed, knowing what must be done, and watched the man pull the maiden apron from the girl's clothing pile and use it to wipe himself off before hurriedly dressing. He stopped at the door and listened, while I shrank back into the shadows. I no longer wished to be seen or acknowledged. I no longer wished to worship at his side.

The man slipped into the darkened alley and retreated toward home.

I followed.

I had gotten very good at shadowing the man, and this was my finest hour. Along the way, I stopped to grab a brick, which had fallen from a crumbling alley wall. The sun was coming up, and the first-shift workers began to fill the streets. I quickened my pace and shortened the distance between us, hiding among the normalcy of quick feet and tired morning eyes.

When the man opened his door, he had not expected me to be right behind him. He was not prepared to be shoved inside. The brick in my hand rendered him unconscious before he could turn and see who was assaulting him within his own walls.

I stood above him for a long while. The scene I'd witnessed

played over and over in my mind. I was disgusted. Not in what he'd done, but in my willingness and naïve belief he could have ever been worthy. The Count would have fed on him, and had he not fallen in the dark cellars of Carfax Abbey, I would have gleefully watched him do so.

I debated what to do until the streets grew quiet, as the workers had all made their way toward the businesses of The East End. I laughed a close-mouthed chuckle to myself at the poetry of it, as I reached down and grabbed the man's own knife to use against him. I lay open his arms, from wrists to elbows, and waited.

The blood pooled underneath him, as it had his victims, but there was no beauty in it. As it spread, I backed away, avoiding the life escaping him. His final exhale was neither exciting nor tragic. It simply was.

I gave his room a perfunctory search and was surprised to find a thick handful of quid — and an idea I hadn't realized was stewing. I'd been hearing chatter of the upcoming World's Fair. When added to my own savings, I would have enough for a steerage ticket on the next steamship.

The time had come to leave London behind. Perhaps Chicago would provide a master rather than a madman.

**Kelli Owen** is a member of both the Horror Writers Association and the International Thriller Writers, and has spoken at the CIA Headquarters in Langley, VA regarding both her writing and the field in general. The author of over a dozen books, including *The HeadlessBoy*, *Teeth*, and the Wilted Lily YA series, her short fiction has appeared in Bram Stoker Award-nominated anthologies alongside Neil Gaiman, Stephen King, Robert McCammon, F. Paul Wilson, and Josh Malerman, among others. Born and raised in Wisconsin, she now lives in the dark woods of Pennsylvania. For more information, please visit her website at kelliowen.com

# Don't Mess With a Renfield

## By Henry Herz

Saturday, I woke with a smile and stretched, looking forward to a long-overdue vacation day. My boss was a successful, highly sought-after paranormal detective, and I didn't get much time off. He possessed remarkable abilities, though he no longer went by the name Dracula. And in the twenty-first century, he no longer stalked strangers. Rather, he preferred to challenge his intellect by solving occult crimes. I was the latest generation in a long line of faithful Renfields serving the former prince of darkness. My master judiciously sipped my blood weekly, giving him all the nourishment he needed, while leaving me human.

My staycation began with a morning at a park with a venti espresso roast, reading Jemisin's *The Fifth Season.* I paid no mind to joggers and dog-walkers, but flirted mid-morning with a cute brunette who sat at my park bench with her laptop. Being a solid six-feet-tall and blonde with blue eyes helped me in that regard.

In the early afternoon, I returned home, took a well-earned nap, and lifted weights. Emerging from the shower, I threw on some sweats and ordered a New York style pizza with spinach, artichokes, and jalapeños.

After tipping the delivery guy, I set the pizza on the living room coffee table and grabbed a beer from the refrigerator.

Turning on the wall-mounted 4K flat screen TV, I surfed through the streaming offerings, stopping at *Dune*. The latest version of that movie had been out for a while, but my lord worked me hard, pushing my recreational viewing far behind schedule.

While being Dracula's assistant was demanding and dangerous, it paid well. Very well. That's how a retired Army Ranger like me could afford a Jaguar F-TYPE and a modern, four-bedroom house with a home gym and lap pool on two acres of secluded woodlands in upstate New York. On the other hand, being Dracula's loyal assistant came with considerable drawbacks, most notably that his successes earned him, and therefore me, powerful enemies — the enemies who survived, anyway.

The sun set. As I finished my beer, the actor portraying Paul Atreides delivered the classic line, "Fear is the mind-killer." My mobile phone buzzed as I reached for a third slice of pizza. *There is motion at camera three*, read the security camera notification.

*Probably a deer,* I thought, engrossed in the movie.

As I took another bite of pizza, my phone buzzed again. Sigh. I pulled up the live video feed for camera three.

*Damn.*

What appeared to be four men in dark clothing moved through the trees toward the southwest corner of my house. They held pistols and wore black balaclavas, leaving only their eyes visible.

*Think! Do I call the police? No. It'll be too late by the time they get here.*

I raced into my office and tapped in the combination to my five-foot-tall gun safe. After throwing on my Ranger Body Armor vest, I slapped on my Ops Core high cut helmet, with an AN/PVS-31 binocular night vision device attached. I shoved a thirteen-round magazine into my Glock pistol and grabbed two more magazines.

To deny my attackers access to the rest of my arsenal, I eased the gun safe closed. I dashed to the wall-mounted circuit breaker panel and shut off power to the house lights. Yes, that tipped off my attackers that they'd lost the element of surprise. Still, they didn't have BNVDs, and that, combined with my familiarity with the floor plan, gave me a tactical advantage.

My camera feeds revealed a pair of intruders approaching the back patio, while a second pair stood ready to breach the garage side door. *Good. Even after you get through that door, there's another locked door between the garage and the house. That'll give me time to neutralize the first pair.*

Switching on my BNVD, I crawled from my office to the living room, halting behind the leather sofa with only my head extending beyond the side. My clear view through the sliding glass door of the back patio showed one of the assassins reaching for the door handle. *It's locked, asshole.* With the house lights off, the moonless night rendered me nearly invisible.

One of them raised a phone to his face. Since they knew that I knew things were about to get violent, they didn't have to worry about noise alerting me. They shot out the glass patio door and charged into my living room. Muffled thumping from the direction of the garage told me the other men were breaching that door.

Once they entered my home, I could legally shoot them in self-defense. *I didn't invite you in.* I smiled grimly.

One of the men slid toward the kitchen. The other advanced into the living room, his pistol at the ready.

I put two rounds in living room guy's chest, and he tumbled backward into my leather La-Z-Boy recliner.

Kitchen guy spun at the sound of my shots and fired off three return rounds. He couldn't see me, but by sheer luck one bullet whizzed dangerously close.

*You better not have hit my new TV, jerkweed.* I put a round through his head.

More thumping from the garage, louder than before, told me the other pair were kicking in the door from the garage to the house. I slipped soundlessly behind the well-stocked wet bar, which offered concealment and a view down the hallway to the garage.

No sooner had I done so, than the remaining attackers burst into the corridor. One of them swept a flashlight beam until he found me, but I put two rounds in his torso, and he went down. My third round hit the other assassin in the thigh as he dived left from the hallway into the laundry room. A room with no other exit.

"Phase one failed. Execute phase two immediately…I know, but you have to advance the schedule," emanated from the laundry room, followed by a smashing sound.

*What the hell is phase two?* I turned my gaze to the man lying prone in the hallway. His abdominal wounds were likely fatal, but it never pays to take chances. From behind the wet bar, I sent a bullet through his chin and out the top of his head. Capturing the last, desperate man would entail risk, but I had to find out who sent them. If someone's pissed off enough to send hitmen, they're likely willing to send more to finish the job.

I switched tactics and called out, "Listen. I knew you were coming and armed myself. So, unless you want me to lob a grenade in there, you'll come out with your hands empty and above your head. You don't want to die, and I don't want to have to buy a new washer and dryer."

*I don't have a grenade, but you don't know that.*

"You shot my leg pretty bad. I can't stand up," came the tremulous response.

"Then toss your gun into the hallway and raise your hands." To give myself the advantage of surprise in case he planned treachery, I advanced quickly and soundlessly toward the laundry room. When his pistol tumbled onto the hallway floor, I stole a rapid glance through the doorway.

He sat on the floor with his back to the far wall, hands pressing his left thigh. A smashed mobile phone lay on the floor between his legs. Blood flowed from his wound into a growing puddle. "I need medical help."

I leaned past the edge of the door just enough to expose my head and hand gripping my Glock. "After you tell me who sent you." The pool of blood grew larger. "You might want to use your belt as a tourniquet to stop the bleeding."

*You're going into shock. I must've hit the femoral artery.*

He winced in agony as he unfastened his belt and struggled to pull it off his waist. "Iä Dagon cf'ayak'vulgtmm, vugtlagln vulgtmm," he chanted.

I scowled. "I don't speak gibberish. If you want help, tell me who sent you."

The man's head lolled to the side, and his hands slid off his belt.

Advancing, I placed two fingers on his wrist.

*He's gone.* His smashed phone prevented me from viewing the number he called. *Crap.*

I strode back to the office and flipped on the circuit breakers to illuminate the house. Deactivating my BNVD, I returned to laundry man for a closer inspection. The color of his blood seemed odd — too brown. On the off chance the assassin had poor tradecraft, I checked his pockets for clues, but they were empty. Removing his balaclava, I rocked back on my heels in revulsion.

His narrow balding head featured a downturned, thick-lipped mouth, small ears, flat nose, and watery-blue bulging eyes. Yellow hairs straggled in irregular patches from grayish cheeks. Scabrous folds lined both sides of his neck.

I cursed at the disturbingly familiar sight.

*Deep One Hybrids!*

These fish/frog humanoids, offspring of accursed matings between humans and Deep Ones, worshipped the Old God, Dagon. Last year, my master and I stopped a group of them from kidnapping women for use as unwilling mates.

*You came for revenge.* My gut twisted.

*Master! If they tried to kill me, they're likely gunning for my lord too. Was that phase two?*

Yanking out my phone, I dialed Dracula's number. No answer.

*Damnit.*

Powerful as he is, he can't abide garlic and crosses.

*At least it's still dark. He'd be much weaker during the day.*

The police weren't an option, as I'd received inviolable orders to never bring others to Dracula's home. I bunched my fists.

*It's up to me to help him.*

Rushing back to my gun safe, I strapped a holster on my thigh. I swapped a new magazine into my Glock and loaded my vest with two more. I grabbed my Colt M4 carbine and slammed in a magazine holding thirty 5.56mm rounds. What it lacked in caliber, the M4 more than made up for in range, rate of fire, and accuracy. I tucked three more carbine magazines and two M67 fragmentation grenades into my vest.

*Fortune favors the prepared.*

Still wearing my body armor and helmet, I grabbed my keyring and sprinted for the garage. My car's rear wheels spewed driveway dirt as I raced toward my master's walled estate, roughly twenty minutes away as the Jag drives. Repeated attempts to reach him by phone failed. Luckily, the roads were empty except for one car I narrowly avoided hitting. I ignored the horn blaring behind me, trying to come up with a plan.

*The other assassins will assume I'm coming.*

A half-mile from Dracula's home, I stopped my car, and used my phone to access my lord's security camera feeds. The wrought-iron entry gates lay bent and broken on the gravel driveway.

*They must've used plastic explosives on the hinges.*

I checked the other security cameras. The torn-apart bodies of three Deep One hybrids lay on the rear lawn, two more on the left side of the house.

*I guess you didn't know about the claymore mines.*

Checking all the cameras, I spotted the assassins waiting to ambush me. Two lay on the grass inside the ten-foot-tall stone perimeter wall, about fifteen yards from the right side of the entry. A third crouched with a rifle on the second-floor balcony facing the gate.

*My lord needs me.*

After some quick preparations, I executed my assault.

My car rolled down the gently sloping driveway toward the destroyed gate. After it passed through, rapid pistol fire tore holes in the right side of the Jaguar while, at a slower rate, bullets punched through the windshield. My master is immune to gunfire, but sadly, I am not.

Luckily, I wasn't in the car. I crouched on the opposite side of the wall from the two hybrids. Once they opened fire, I tossed a grenade over the wall and hurried to take up a position just outside the entry. When the grenade detonated, I sidestepped from behind the wall and emptied half a clip from my carbine at the remaining assassin. The balcony balusters did not provide full cover for him, and even where they partially shielded him from view, they failed to stop the M995 52-grain armor-piercing bullets with tungsten cores.

I took one step forward and glanced to my right to confirm the first two guys were down. One had a shredded face and the other was missing an arm.

My pockmarked Jag rolled to a halt at the courtyard's stone fountain, where a bronze dragon sprayed water, seeming to celebrate the newly wrought death and destruction. The mansion's ornately carved oak front doors lay splintered, blown off their hinges. I sprinted for the opening.

*They must know my master can shape-shift into mist to avoid being found, so they're probably headed for his coffin. If they steal the Transylvanian soil that sustains him, that will end him as surely as a wooden stake through the heart!*

I raced up the veined marble front steps and across the broken threshold into the darkness. A grim smile appeared on my face.

*My lord must have shut off his lights like I did.*

The attackers would likely search for my master's coffin in the basement. He kept it in the attic, accessible only by a staircase hidden behind a sliding section of the ebony board and batten paneling in his second-floor study.

Shouldering my carbine, I removed another grenade from my vest. I glided to the kitchen, where stairs led down to the basement. No sounds echoed up the steps. Using my BNVD, I confirmed the cellar held no intruders.

*They must be upstairs. Not good.*

I stowed the grenade and unshouldered my carbine. Creeping up the grand curving staircase, I halted five steps from the top. I eased myself forward, exposing just enough of my head to see.

A flashlight beam illuminated the far end of the sixty-foot hallway. Eight balaclava-clad figures moved slowly toward me. The two in front brandished silver crosses, one of whom also carried the flashlight. Crossbows swung awkwardly from their belts.

*No doubt armed with wooden quarrels to serve as flying stakes.*

Behind the cross-bearers trudged four hybrids carrying bulging sacks.

*The dirt from Dracula's coffin! How did they know where to look?*

Two more cross-bearing hybrids brought up the rear.

*My master can't snap their necks if he can't approach. But if he materializes, they will stake him. Clever bastards.*

I took aim. My first shot shattered the flashlight. I ducked down as the two men in front drew pistols and fired wildly in the darkness. When their guns clicked on empty magazines, I rose and shot one of the hybrids in the head, the other in the chest.

The two hybrids with crosses at the rear of the group quickly advanced to the front, exchanging their crosses for flashlights and pistols. A shot whizzed by my left ear, and I backed down two stairs.

*Crap. These two are better trained than the others. If I rise up to shoot one, the other will nail me. I've got one grenade left, but I don't know if the blast will spoil the soil.*

Screams and vampiric snarls interrupted my train of thought. Bodies tumbled to the carpet with muffled thuds.

I risked a peek. The four soil-bearing hybrids lay twisted and broken on the carpet.

*My lord must have materialized behind the group.*

One of the two surviving cross-bearers turned and forced my lord back by brandishing his cross with one hand and fumbling for his crossbow with the other. The man in front reminded me to take shorter peeks by snapping off two rounds, one of which punched through my upper left bicep. It wasn't life-threatening, but it hurt like hell.

I ducked back. Knowing Dracula is unaffected by mundane weapons, I decided to try an inelegant tactic that would have made my old master sergeant scowl. Keeping my head and torso out of the hybrid's line of fire, I raised the carbine above my head and fired blindly. Fifteen rounds later, my gun clicked empty, and I slapped in another magazine.

"You can come up now, Renfield."

I stood and saw my random fire had killed the last two men. Relief washed over me, and I temporarily forgot I was leaking blood. "I'm glad you're safe, my lord."

Dracula smiled. "Thank you. Let us adjourn to the kitchen, away from those crosses, so I may dress your wound."

His sense of smell where blood was concerned was better than, dare I say it, a bloodhound's. The look of disgust on his face when striding past his attackers told me their brownish befouled blood would not be to his taste.

He sat me down in the kitchen and inspected my wound. "It appears you are in luck — the bullet struck no bone." He cleaned and dressed my injury with the dexterity of a surgeon. My efforts even earned me a shot of painkiller. "Would you like a cold beer? I keep a six-pack of Bergenbier on hand for your visits."

Normally, I'd be the one fixing him drinks, often a Bloody Mary. Despite being a prince of darkness, he had a sense of humor. I felt too exhausted and thirsty to insist. "Thank you, my lord."

He smiled. "No, it is I who should thank you. Their clever plan to use crosses to keep me at bay whilst they stole my Transylvanian soil would have worked had it not been for your cleverness and courage. I am deeply in your debt."

Maybe it was the painkiller talking, but I replied. "That's great, master, because I could use a new Jaguar…and another day off."

**Author's Notes**

Deep One hybrid creatures appeared in H.P. Lovecraft's stories *Dagon* (1919) and *The Shadow over Innsmouth* (1931). These foul creatures faced off previously against Dracula and Renfield on a cruise ship in the story, *Norsemen Cruise Line*, Dracula Beyond Stoker issue #1 (2022).

Renfield's relationship with Dracula offers subtle pathos. Per Dracula canon, the vampire exercises mind control over those from whom he drinks blood. But Renfield doesn't realize that, thinking he serves his master of his own free will.

The mention of Bergenbier, a Romanian beer brand, is a wink at Dracula's Transylvanian heritage.

**Henry Herz**'s speculative fiction short stories include "Norsemen Cruise Line" (*Dracula Beyond Stoker* #1), "Out, Damned Virus" (*Daily Science Fiction*), "Bar Mitzvah on Planet Latke" (*Coming of Age,* Albert Whitman & Co.), "The Magic Backpack" (*Metastellar*), "Unbreakable" (*Musing of the Muses*, Brigid's Gate Press), "A Vampire, an Astrophysicist, and a Mother Superior Walk Into a Basilica" (*Three Time Travelers Walk Into...*, Fantastic Books), "The Case of the Murderous Alien" (*Spirit Machine*, Air and Nothingness Press), "Maria & Maslow" (*Highlights for Children*), and "A Proper Party" (*Ladybug Magazine*). He's edited five anthologies and written twelve picture books, including the critically acclaimed *I Am Smoke*. www.henryherz.com

# R.N.
## By Amelia Mangan

Most human beings are born between the hours of midnight and dawn.

This is one of the first things the older nurses tell you, when you begin your training in this field. There is a kind of fascinated awe in their voices when they relate this fact to you, as though they themselves cannot fathom why such a thing should be. They look at you expectantly, anticipating queries, assuming you — especially as a man, a tourist on this blood-soaked terrain — are as curious as they, regarding this phenomenon. They assume you will have questions. They assume you will wonder why.

I never wonder why.

Another night shift has begun, and I am armed and ready. My scrubs are washed and pressed, only the faintest scent of afterbirth detectible within the fine-woven threads. My hands wrap around a paper cup of coffee. The cardboard is too thin and the substance inside burns my palms, but this is part of it, this helps also. In my pocket, a plastic bag of brightly colored pills — no more than my height and weight require — shifts with the movements of my body. I find I am hyperconscious of my breath at times like this, the laborious manner in which my lungs claw it from the air and hold it and expel it, a pump that never ceases, until someday it does.

I am one of the only male nurses on the ward at this, the busiest hour of the night. Nurse Lind once told me in confidence that this is because the presence of too many men sometimes makes the laboring women uncomfortable. I said I doubted that I could make the women any more uncomfortable than their own men already had. Joking, of course. Nurse Lind didn't laugh, only looked at me.

I suppose they would prefer to get along without me if it were possible. Nurse Lind would prefer that. But it isn't possible. I am needed. It is a powerful thing, to know that you are needed.

Six women sit in the emergency room now. Thickened ankles planted on rubber flooring, swollen hands gripped by hapless males, unable to grasp that their role in this play is over. Bovine, *he* once called these women, back when he was able. I suppose it makes a certain amount of sense that he would view them that way, as cattle.

He had his own women, of course, back in the old country. Three of them. Not like *these* women, not at all. A different breed. Strange, sphinxlike creatures, gliding through stone corridors on feet that bore no weight. Totally hairless, as far as I could tell. In my sojourns throughout the castle I would sometimes encounter them, drifting down the hallways like torn shreds of cobweb. They never seemed to see me, and I never learned where they were going. I preferred not to think of them, then. I prefer not to think of them now. The castle was a long time ago.

Now the women in my world are akin to the one who has just this minute arrived, crashing through the double doors, splayed on a gurney: loud and red-faced, sweaty and moaning. Hair plastered to flushed skin. Stomach distended like those of starving children, navel a tumor in toad-belly flesh. The women of the castle had skin like glass, so thin you could see the empty network of veins within, hollow and flat. These women display their veins also, popping and straining inside their necks, but there is nothing empty about them.

So much blood inside these women. So much *life.*

And it is my job (not my duty, no, I *know* my duty, and it lies elsewhere within this hospital; but my job, nevertheless) to assist these women in their titanic struggles with the life inside them, with that which rends and tears them from within. I have seen the damage inflicted upon them by that which their bodies house: raw red slits ripped beyond even their impressive elastic capabilities, pelvic bones shattered that the infant may be pulled from the wreckage, a caesarian section's gaping razor grin. Some come dangerously close to bleeding to death. A terrible waste. I try to salvage what I can, but being under observation, this can prove difficult.

Luckily, we are understaffed tonight. Which is nothing new. *Budget cuts,* Nurse Lind likes to proclaim with gloomy mien to nobody in particular, but most often, it seems, to me. She usually says this upon discovering an absence of some resource when we are taking inventory: a low supply of morphine, for instance, or intravenous tubing, or colostomy bags, or brightly colored pills.

Things go missing around here, sometimes. There are disappearances. Internal investigations, privately conducted. Incidents, quietly handled.

*Budget cuts.* Nurse Lind says it in a tone that suggests she is explaining something to herself.

I have already taken two pills tonight, before my arrival. I am prepared. I am on my feet, though I do not recall standing, and I am beside the wailing woman, hurtling down the corridor under the bright fluorescent glare of the lights. Nurse Lind has tried to have these lights removed; she claims they interfere with our patients' circadian rhythms, those complex interplays of nature and biology whereby rest and relief from pain may be found in darkness. I wonder if such concerns matter much to *him* anymore. I assume he would let me know somehow. He can bear it, in any event.

Oh, my mind wanders, it *wanders,* and I must have focus. Perhaps the pills were a mistake. I have lost weight recently. It was *he* who demanded I first start taking the pills, long ago, seeing my frail and human struggles with wakefulness during the hours when he had most need of me. *You must have focus,* those were his words. He was old, did not understand the manner in which the drug interacted with my body chemistry, did not care to learn;

only knew there was a way for me to disregard sleep, to cast off my own circadian rhythms, retune them to his frequency. And I did it, of course I did it. By then, I'd given up greater things than sleep for him.

I understand such things are necessary. I know my purpose, know that it is to serve. I bear no malice.

The vastness of the woman is hauled off the gurney, all groans and gusting breaths. Blood and amniotic fluid slick the insides of her thighs. I slip on mask and gloves and prepare the epidural as Doctor Fleming and Nurse Lind rush past and around me, flying gowns brushing at my cheek like the fluttering wings of bats. Talk reverberates in my ear, low-voiced concern: *possible breach, three months premature.*

There is a tank, unused, in the corner of this room. Sometimes we have water births here. Children born into blood, my hands immersed in lukewarm water and shredded uterine tissue, up to the wrists, the forearms. And all the while knowing it lurks: that great gaping mouth under the lurching waves.

I see it now, in the stretch-marked shadow of her belly, between the bonelike knobs of her knees: the raw red sideways smile, dark fur and swollen meat. A fangless carnivore, and what good, I wonder, is a carnivore without fangs? How can it defend itself? How can it survive?

"Check the dilation," Doctor Fleming urges me. I am taken aback. This task normally does not fall to me, but we are short-staffed (*budget cuts*) and so I do it, of course I do it. My fingers sink into the maw, shielded by only the thinnest of latex, and as they quest at the neck of the womb (the neck, always the neck) a tiny heartbeat convulsion draws from me a startled breath: a fetal hand grabs at my finger, five little spiders' legs wrapping about my gloved flesh.

I withdraw my hand and report that dilation is at ten centimeters. Birth will occur at any moment. I still feel the hand around my finger, the pinprick pulse beating at my knucklebone.

Three months premature. It is possible the child will not live.

My mind roams the hospital corridors, away from here, beyond the beds of howling women and the cots of comatose infants; into the quiet halls of sleep, the private rooms, private Room 7-D which no one but I may enter or exit, in which the very private patient is cordoned off by a gauzy curtain. The name on the form — filled out by hand, my unrecognizable left hand - reads only "JOHN DOE", his condition "CONFIDENTIAL". The room is expensive, as are all the private rooms. The patient can afford it. I am the one who pays.

The door is locked, always. Only I hold the key. My hand — the hand the child held — drifts up to my collar, touches the silver chain around my neck. The chain twists beneath my sullied scrubs, and the key hangs against my naked flesh, cold against my heart.

Only I hold the key. Only I.

The woman is unconscious now, slack face hidden by a screen. Doctor Fleming has spread her legs apart in struts of steel. She is all body, all distended fangless mouth, straining to disgorge that which sticks in the throat, in the neck. All ragged, gaping hole.

It is better, I think, if I cannot see the face.

At my back, a sound of squeaking rubber. I glance over my shoulder. Two orderlies, little mayflies, buzz around the incubator they have wheeled into the room. A tiny, delicate glass coffin, threaded through with tubes and wiring.

I kept *him* in a coffin, at first. Filled with bloodied earth, the earth of his homeland. He insisted upon it, even after we had left that homeland for good, even after I had told him how difficult it would be to obtain such an object without arousing suspicion. He did not care. Berated me for even daring to voice such timid objections. Raged at me. I remember his rages, back then, back when he still was able to rage. So towering, so terrible. I remember feeling so afraid.

Later, while recovering, I came to understand my error. The coffin was traditional, after all. The way things were done, had always been done. He only ever wanted to do things the way they had always been done. A very old man, born and bred to the demands of aristocracy, of hierarchy. Everything in its proper place.

Doctor Fleming's hands are deep inside the woman. I can see them working beneath the skin of her abdomen. Blood froths around the doctor's wrists, slops onto the linen beneath. There is a scent of iron on the air, laced with discharge and shit, the smell thick enough to penetrate my mask; it mingles in my mouth with the staleness of my own breath.

An arm, purple in hue, flops out of the woman. Five little fingers. All so much smaller and thinner than they ought to be.

When *his* right arm went gangrenous — liquid silver, poured out upon the fingers by (I informed him) zealous hunters, those who thought, in foolish hope, to harm him — it was I who suggested that we amputate. The infection, I reasoned, would almost certainly spread, and his immune system was of such ancient vintage that it could not possibly handle the task on its own. He was reluctant, but this, I reminded him, was what his ancestors had always done, when dealing with such malignancy; what he himself had seen done on the battlefield, in his human days, as a mighty general. This reassured him, calmed him. He allowed me to perform my duty.

As it happened, the infection had spread already. After much consideration, I decided to remove his other arm, too. Pre-emptive, perhaps, but I would have been remiss in my duty had I not taken care of him.

The baby slithers out of the woman and into Doctor Fleming's hands. A slender piece of gristle, riding a red-white wave. It is no bigger than Doctor Fleming's palm; he scarcely requires both in which to cradle it. Its limbs are insectoid, its head a blue-tinged bobbin on a stalk of a neck. It does not cry, does not look as though it possesses strength enough to cry.

Doctor Fleming hands the still little form off to Nurse Lind, waiting with fresh cloth, clean dressings. She towels off the afterbirth, sets the baby down, begins to massage the skeleton ribs, to press life and breath into the flattened, fluid-filled lungs.

Its eyelids are translucent. I can see the blind black pupils underneath.

The purpose of a small life is to provide strength to the larger life within which it dwells. Spiders eat flies. Rats eat spiders. Cats eat rats. The woman would have been better off keeping the infant inside her. Everyone would have been better off.

*You should have stayed inside,* I think. *You would have been safe inside.*

The chest rises, falls, does not rise again; but a pulse is detected, the most delicate of threads. The glass coffin is opened, the tiny body placed inside. Tubes are connected, monitors flash.

The child lives. It almost certainly will not live, but it lives.

The key to Room 7-D beats against my chest. I am going to have to perform my duty.

I promised him I would. When the next set of hunters shattered his legs with stakes of iron, hammered into the joints while he slept (again it fell to me to inform him of this outrage), it became clear to us both that he could no longer seek nourishment on his own. Once, he could've commanded his women to hunt for him. But the women were gone. There had been a fire, he remembered that; a fire that took the castle, forced us to leave the old country. Someone had set the fire on purpose. I reminded him that the hunters had done this, too. He had begun to forget so many things by then. A great pity.

I have forgotten things, also. I cannot remember my mother. I cannot remember anything before *him*, taking me as his own, as servant. He has made of me an empty chalice.

I take a breath behind my mask and head toward the incubator, commandeering it from the orderlies. "I'll take this to NICU," I say, keeping my voice fixed in steady nonchalance.

Nurse Lind, standing at the woman's side, sponging sweat from her invisible brow, looks up sharply. Her eyes gleam hard behind her glasses. As though, perhaps, she sees something.

"I'll take care of it," she says, bustling over, nudging me aside with the barest of pressure, as if not wishing to touch me any more than necessary.

"It's fine," I say, not relinquishing my hold. "You're needed here."

"Not really," she says. "Just clean-up now, basically. You can handle that." Her voice is just as carefully calibrated, as challenging in its casual neutrality, as mine.

A child went missing from the NICU, early in September. A child very much like this one. Barely alive, almost no brain function at all. Attached to machines, a thousand tubes and wires invading its unresponsive flesh, biting into it, drawing blood. Nobody expected it to survive the night. It would have served no purpose, keeping it alive.

I was on the ward that night, too.

I did make him a promise. I understand that I must keep it. I must keep that which I have made.

"She's going to need stitches," I say, nodding over my shoulder toward Doctor Fleming. "Could be complications. You're probably better off supervising."

"No, it's standard procedure," says Nurse Lind. "Just have to make her comfortable, that's all. But ,"She wrests the incubator from my hand,"*this* little guy's gonna need all-night supervision. You don't want to have to do that."

"I'm used to all-nighters," I say, but my voice has grown enfeebled, lacking conviction. There is some comfort in this, in the knowledge that this is now out of my hands. That I have a reasonable excuse for not performing my duty in *this* manner.

"Just take care of the mess," says Nurse Lind, steering the incubator away from me. "Clean her up. Get an early night. You look like you could use a rest." Her bland eyes stare me down. "Maybe you should think about laying off all that…coffee."

I shift my stance. The pills in my pocket shift with me.

"I'll clean her up," I say.

Nurse Lind nods. Her eyes remain on me. I feel them even after she has turned away, after the incubator has rolled through the door and out of sight.

I turn back to the bed. Doctor Fleming is stitching up the torn flesh traversing the woman's holes, sealing up the ravaged gateway. It always strikes me as strange, this notion that one type of hole in a woman's flesh is normal, natural, and another type an error that requires correction. Why stitch up that which is already laid open? How does one distinguish wound from wound?

The placenta has sluiced out onto the linen. A slab of rare beef, veined with dark blue streaks. The first food any of us will ever know, the food that is of another's body, another's blood. Sometimes the women keep it, store it in a refrigerator, like wedding cake. A mark of achievement, a symbol of power, of one's ability to feed and to consume. I wrap it in white cloth, swaddled like a second infant, and place it to one side.

The hole is closed now. Doctor Fleming moves aside and allows me to lift the woman's bloodied hips, change out the linens beneath them. Sterile sponge dipped in warm water. I swab out her inner thighs, her rough-sewn pubis, as best as I am able. The water blooms a darker red each time I dip my hand beneath it.

Those five little fingers, wrapped about my hand. I feel them still.

A quick swipe across the forehead and the woman is as clean as I can make her. Blankets are drawn over hips, a curtain falling, the play is over. Doctor Fleming leaves and I am alone. I reach over the prone body before me and gather up the placenta in my arms. I hold it very gently, dimming the lights as I go. The woman breathes deep and slow, easeful at her drugged rest. She knows nothing, feels nothing. An unexpected wave of tenderness toward her overtakes me as I leave, a kind of gratitude.

There is no one in the break room when I enter. Short-staffed. Everyone on call. A paper cup of coffee rests on the table, half-full and hastily abandoned, red lipstick kiss on its rim. I place the bundle on the countertop and unwrap it with the care of a butcher. The lump of flesh looks nourishing, healthy. Hormones and nutrients. Immunity from infection, strengthening of bonds. It looks healthier than the babe it fed.

I pull a knife from the drawer, cut the object to pieces, drop them into the blender, hit puree. The meat whirls and splatters within.

I wonder if the child will survive the night.

The sound it made. Not *this* child. The other child. Early in September. When I brought it home, when I gave it to him, when I lowered it to his maw. That urgent little squall, that very first and very last burst of panic. That liquid sound. That *sucking* sound.

A premature baby that time, too. Why I chose it. A preemie. God, these cute little names we give them. It probably would have died anyway. Probably wouldn't have survived the night. Probably.

This way is better. Better that I bear the responsibility myself. Better that I be the chalice.

I switch off the blender, turn to the table, pick up the discarded cup. Empty the coffee into the sink, rinse off the insides. The lipstick imprint remains intact. Indelible. Designed to be so, I suppose. A kiss that lingers, a scar that remains.

The castle women, they used to bring him babies. Not their own, of course. Once, passing by a shuttered room, I glimpsed the youngest naked, changing her bloodied clothing. She had nothing between her legs. No holes, only sealed flesh. But she brought him babies. Wherever it was those women went, passing me silently by in those stone hallways, they always returned with babies. I went to sleep with those babies' cries in my ears. Almost normal, after a time. The way those cries grew frantic, the way they cut off so abruptly. The gurgling sounds. The sucking sounds.

I was young, then. How young? Teenaged, perhaps. It seems long ago, but my perception sometimes lies to me. I do not like to look in my own eyes, but I catch sight of myself in the mirror over the sink, washing out the cup, trailing my thumb across the stained paper rim. It shocks me to see that I still look young. Tired, yes. Silver threads in my hair, like chains. But young. Nobody would guess at the life I have lived. Nobody would ever know.

The cup is as clean as I can make it. I place it on the counter and pour the liquefied meat inside, up to the limit. Screw the plastic lid back on and take a sip. The drink is frothy and warm, like heated milk. It bites at the back of my throat. Rests, metallic, on my tongue. Perhaps it will save me from infection, too.

I wash the blender, dry it off. Wad up the bloody cloth and stuff it into my pocket. Take the coffee cup and wander back out into the hallway, following its twists and curves, until I am away from the maternity unit, until the women and their preemies and all their chorused cries are far behind me.

Hours to go before the dawn. I wonder how many babies will be born before the dark draws back. How many little lives, once so safe inside that larger life, will find themselves thrust cold and howling into the indifferent night.

I drink from my cup.

The corridors in the private sector are quiet, empty. The lighting here is low. Nurse Lind would like it. All around, one senses breath, deep and slow, each exhalation counting down the midnight hours. To breathe here is to breathe sleep. There is little worry in the private rooms. No expectation of sudden awakening, of being told that the bed in which they make their rest must be vacated. Only safety here.

I drink from my cup.

When I moved him into the hospital, into Room 7-D, late in September, I laid out the facts as cleanly as I could. By then I had amputated his legs, too — no choice, you see; the iron had poisoned his flesh; had to be done — so he had little option but to listen. I told him I could no longer keep him at my apartment, that people had noticed the scattered earth around my door, that the coffin was too large for the space, that the landlady had asked me about a baby's cry. I told him of the equipment we had here, that it was state-of-the-art, only the very best for him. I told him how many times per night the nurses here performed their rounds. I told him that there was always a chance, no matter how minute, that the key might fall out of my possession and into the hands of another. I told him how loudly he moaned in his sleep, reminded him how often he dreamed of his phantom limbs, how past pain and present hunger led his vocal cords to betray him without his knowledge. I told him what had to be done. What was necessary, for both our survival. I reassured him, even as I took the bone saw to his neck, even as he cried out and tried to squirm away, that I would take care of him, always. Was this not my duty?

My cup is almost empty. I am almost there. The meat churns inside my gut. Hormones and nutrients. I extract a pill from my pocket, pop it into my mouth. I drink from my cup.

Normally I try not to take too many pills right before his feeding. It keeps him awake. Up all night, just like me. But there are times, like tonight, when I feel that this is fitting.

That *sucking* sound. I think of it so often.

I am at the door. Room 7-D. I press my ear to the wood. The soothing hum of machinery, the muted beep of a monitor. Not a heart monitor, of course. Just the vitals, the parts he cannot do without. He hasn't had a working heart in a very long time.

I fish my key from beneath my shirt, slot it in. With gentle hands, on soft feet, I push the door inward.

The room is pitched in darkness, all but drowned in it. Others would have trouble; I can see just fine. The bower of the curtain, the lumped and half-formed outline, black on black. The sound of something wet.

I shut the door, move into the room, stand at the foot of the bed. I look in on him.

I drink from my cup. Drain it to the dregs.

He lies, bare and unclothed, in a nest of tubes and wires. No arms, no legs. Where the head once was, not even so much as a stump. My cuts are very clean.

A catheter is threaded through the nub of his penis, a colostomy bag heavy with molten shit hangs from his bloated abdomen. Strange, I think, that he should possess these holes, where the castle women had none. It seems unfair somehow.

His torso is a rat-queen of veins, deflated beneath the skin. Initially I had thought to feed him intravenously, but those veins, those ancient highways and byways, could not withstand such heavy traffic. The entire infrastructure collapsed. That was when I thought to open the ventral cavity. Directly expose the digestive tract, feed him that way. Cut out the middleman.

The slit down his torso is raw and red and very, very wet. I would not have thought that someone so pallid, so bloodless, could contain such vivid red. One never really knows what's going on inside another person.

I wonder if he feels pain. I wonder if he knows what pain is. What the word even means. Does he know words, now? Does he think? Does he still dream? Does he everdream of me?

What I do not wonder, never wonder, is why he carries on. Why he does not die. What kind of will could possibly keep such a creature alive?

I know exactly what kind of will could accomplish that.

I crush the cup in my hand and move in toward him.

"It's been a very long night, my master," I say. "I imagine you must be hungry."

Although I cannot know if he hears me — how it is that he possibly could — the slit in his chest begins to pulsate. The sides of the wound, the fleshy pink lips, press together and come apart with a soft wet smack. The sucking sound.

Most nights, I feed him by mouth, as a mother bird might. My stomach acids break down the meat, make it easier for him to digest. And there is a certain symmetry in feeding him this way, he who once deployed his mouth as a weapon, as instrument of enslavement. This symmetry pleases me. I am, after all, trained to spot that which is in disarray, that which requires smoothing out. I alleviate unnecessary suffering. That is my duty.

Tonight, however, a certain amount of suffering may be necessary. A little labor on his part.

I roll up my left sleeve. The suction marks are still visible, from last time, but the scars are all but healed.

I stand over him, my arm extended, fingers inches above his wound. The lips sense the proximity, suck at the air.

Five little fingers. Wrapped around mine.

I shove my hand hard and deep into the gash. Deeper. Wrist-deep, forearm-deep. Elbow-deep is as far as I have ever dared go, but the night is young, and endless.

The slit spasms, as though in pain, in shock. After a moment or two, it begins to suck at me. I feel it as a pressure, flesh and muscle against bone, tearing my veins wide open. Last time I fed him this way, he almost broke my wrist, and I did not feed him for three nights after. It is possible that he feels anger toward me, inasmuch as he can feel at all, but of course I bear no malice. I do my duty, and he does only as any child would do.

In these quiet and sacred hours between midnight and dawn, these birthing hours, I am servant, and nurse, and mother. I care for him. I sacrifice. I sustain. And he understands with every un-thinking cell of his body that we are bonded, he and I, chained to one another by an unbreakable cord. He knows now that he could never truly survive without me.

Deep inside him, under the knives of the ribs and close to the withered heart, I curl my five fingers into a fist.

**Amelia Mangan** is an author currently living in Sydney, Australia. Her stories have been featured in a number of publications, including *The Best Horror of the Year Volume 11* (ed. Ellen Datlow), and adapted in audio form by Jason Hill for the hit podcast Chilling Tales for Dark Nights. Her first novel, *Release*, was published by Nightscape Press in 2015.

Updates on her work can be found at http://ameliamangan.substack.com

# TOOTHPICKINGS

# The Ballad of Renfield

*See my lonely life unfold*
*I see it every day*
*See my only mind explode*
*Since I've gone away*
— Alice Cooper, "The Ballad of Dwight Fry"

When Alice Cooper donned a straitjacket to record "The Ballad of Dwight Fry", he was saluting the characters that actor Dwight Frye was known for playing — maniacal, slavish, in need of serious help far beyond what bubble baths and a scalp massage could cover.

A lot of backstory is left untold in Cooper's song: why is Dwight Fry[1] institutionalized? How did he escape? What drove him to this point in his life?

We run into the same problem with the real Dwight Frye's best-known character: Renfield.

That Renfield is an impactful character seems obvious — he's been the model for the vampire familiar just as Dracula has been the model for the vampire for 125 years. We could catalog all the

---

[1]According to some sources, Cooper changed the spelling of Frye's name to avoid legal entanglements. If so, he inadvertently changed the name back to the original, pre-stage name spelling that appears on the great actor's birth certificate.

post-Dracula instances of familiars being disturbed thralls to their detached vampires — from King's Straker to Martin's Sour Billy to Lindqvist's Håkan[2] — but why waste everyone's time with a listicle? We see the Renfield model followed time and again — even when familiars claw back a bit of their humanity, they remain disposable to their undead masters — an image Renfield crystallized.

But how did the Renfield we know in *Dracula* come to be?

Was it an astonishing coincidence that someone under Dracula's power should be committed in an institution next door to Dracula's new digs at Carfax Abbey? I fail to see how that was part of Dracula's plan because: what's the advantage? It's not like Renfield is going to escape his cell and do some light cleaning up around Carfax ahead of his master's arrival. Rather, Renfield is a liability — posing a danger of informing on his boss with as loose as his lips get around Doctor Seward. And indeed, the one plot point Renfield solidly affects is telling on Dracula, in a moment of clarity. If having a mole in Seward's sanitarium was the plan, it was a bad plan.

If the riddle of Renfield is to be solved, it probably will be done by someone who doesn't begin an essay by quoting Alice Cooper. But that scholar is busy chasing tenure, so for now let's see if we can provide a few clues to the critic who will eventually diagnose and cure our collective Renfield quandaries.

## Which Seward Did You Crawl Out Of?

We don't have a lot in Stoker's notes that answers the question "Why Renfield?" However, we do have a few pieces of evidence that might help us answer "How Renfield?"

In the journal Stoker kept in the years long before he started on *Dracula*, we can find a note to himself from 1872 — a memory he perhaps wanted to keep for later exploitation: "I once knew

---

2 Respectively, Stephen King's *Salem's Lot* (1975), George R. R. Martin's *Fevre Dream* (1982), and John Ajvide Lindqvist's *Let The Right One In* (2004)

a little boy who put so many flies into a bottle that they had not room to die!!!"[3]

This memory would show up two decades later when Stoker was scratching out notes for his vampire novel and used the placeholder name "Flyman" for the madman he was developing. He never names his madman in the notes; and he does not audition alternate names. A given name for Flyman must have materialized later.

## Spread Your Wings And Flyman

Whence the name? Some have suggested, as Elizabeth Miller did, that it was inspired by Bertha Rheinfeldt in La Fanu's *Carmilla*. That's a reasonable guess, given how much *Dracula* was inspired by *Carmilla*.

There's also the possibility, offered by Robert Eighteen-Bisang and Elizabeth Miller, that Stoker plucked the name from the Lyceum Theatre's production of *The Strange Case of Dr. Jekyll and Mr. Hyde*, staged while Stoker was ten years into his management career at the theater. One of the narrators of that play is a Mr. Richard Enfield... R. Enfield.

Another possibility is a long road in Glasgow: Renfield Street. Stoker left many footprints on this particular road while traveling through Scotland with the Lyceum Theater and while vacationing in Cruden Bay (where he wrote large portions of *Dracula*). Stoker would have come face-to-face with the name of his madman-in-the-making each and every time he patronized the Theatre Royal in Glasgow, located at the end of Renfield Street.

We never get a satisfactory clue as to what "R.M.", Renfield's first initials, might stand for. "Rat Master", "Rocket Man", "Robert Mueller", and "Royal Majesty" are all equally possible. Stoker appears to have put thought into quite a number of his

---

3 Elizabeth Miller & Dacre Stoker(editors), *The Lost Journal of Bram Stoker,* (Great Britain: The Robson Press, 2012), 66.

character's names; did he do the same for Renfield's full name? Or was "R.M." another placeholder that never got upgraded?

## Outstanding In His Renfield

What thematic or symbolic purpose Renfield serves in the story is some Smart People Stuff. But how he gets into the story, plot wise, is just as much of a head scratcher.

We never get a satisfactory origin story for Renfield. It is suggested that he might have been some sort of gentleman of society, who hobnobbed with Arthur Holmwood's father and was committed to Seward's sanitarium by friends. But beyond that? Opaque. It's no wonder multiple adaptations have grafted histories onto Renfield to connect him to Dracula in more concrete ways.

*Nosferatu* (1922) had Orlock-as-Dracula corrupt the mind of Knock-as-Renfield via letters and symbols. *Dracula* (1931) combined Renfield and Jonathan Harker so as to allow us to watch the devolution of proper-Englishman-to-lunatic under Dracula's power. *Bram Stoker's Dracula* (1992) treated Renfield as an attorney for Peter Hawkins who preceded Harker to Transylvania and was corrupted by Dracula. The BBC's *Dracula* (2020) made Renfield a hired attorney for Dracula's British interests, once again decaying from competent and dry professional to madman. In these cases and others, we get to meet Renfield before he's so far gone, and we get to see how encountering Dracula rots his mind. Mostly, this results in Renfield being a cautionary tale for the heroes of the story: take Dracula seriously or you too will end up like Renfield!

Stoker gives us no such connection.

Unless we want to squint hard. Let's engage in light conjecture:

In *Dracula's Guest*, an unnamed Englishman is traveling through Styria (not yet Transylvania) when he's assaulted on Walpurgis' Night, before being protected by a (were)wolf. It's implied that the wolf is either controlled by — or *is* — Dracula. Hell, the entire assault may have been orchestrated by Dracula for the psychological dividends it would later pay from the Englishman.

Regardless of how conspiratorial one wants to read *Dracula's Guest*, there's a bit that should stand out to us. Because while it's often — reasonably — assumed that the unnamed Englishman is Jonathan Harker; the English narrator of the story speaks almost no German. Harker, in the novel, speaks decent enough German to get by.

So if we accept that there's some continuity with the novel, this means that the Englishman of *Dracula's Guest* is not Jonathan Harker. Could it be Renfield? This would make *Dracula's Guest* the origin story for Renfield. He's terrorized by Dracula, only to be rescued by Dracula. One can imagine the damage to the psyche: being nearly killed by an undead countess only to wake up underneath the tongue of a wolf. Then to learn that your protector was the strange Count? One might understandably form a warped loyalty.[4]

This coffin does not have a bow on it. Remnants of *Dracula's Guest* that somehow didn't get edited out of *Dracula* suggest that the unnamed Englishman was intended to be Harker all along. But the Renfield possibility is tantalizing because it explains the existence of a major character in a way that's lacking.

Harker gets Mina and his sanity, can't Renfield have this?


## The Final Cat

The origins of both Stoker's Renfield and Cooper's Dwight Fry are less than satisfying. It's reasonable that *Dracula* adaptations, wanting to keep this fascinating character, have made efforts to impose an origin onto him so as to create a solid connection between Renfield and Dracula, as well as let Renfield serve as a cautionary tale rather than a madman who exists in a vacuum.

---

[4] Editor's Note: For a fantastic take on this read "Last Days" by Dacre Stoker and Leverett Butts, *Weird Tales no. 364*, 2021

*Dracula* scholars are continuing to dig up new information well over a century after publication; one can hope that information on Renfield will be included in future discoveries.

# FROM THE GRAVE

# Renfield's Wife
## By Damon Cavalchini

It is my mistress's saliva that stops the blood from clotting. Sweet rivers of chemicals intermingling with the other woman's blood, holding back the tide from the wound. Safe in my little wooden hut, surrounded by the protective blanket of the rainforest, no one can hear us. I stand in my appointed corner, feet scraping on the splintering floorboards, watching as the woman thrashes against the knotted ropes that cling, binding her to the eating chair. Ignoring her protests, my mistress continues to feed, on the woman's exposed flesh. The electric hum of desire singing in the air. She's only one person, just another lost tourist. But as we have been living off the local wildlife for the past few months, she is as juicy as any forbidden fruit.

I walk around the edges of the feeding, not wanting to interfere, glancing again at the rough hessian rope, making sure the bulging knots are holding firm. The whole canvas of her skin, not just her face and neck, presents varied opportunities for my mistress's bite. About five foot eight with blond hair and a look of ruffled despair, the woman is another victim of nature's never-ending dance of death and renewal. A lonely traveller kidnapped under the rainforest's tropical shawl.

I rarely see any of my mistress's brothers although I know they exist, chattering away in other parts of the forest. They avoid us, not caring for my presence. Besides, the males don't need the blood, you see. They can survive on the rainforest's rich berries and hunched fruits. It is the females who require the wine of humanity to survive, to breed. Before my eyes the age-old ritual continues, the essential struggle to recreate yourself, to make a family, to survive. Procreate or die.

The woman fights, trying to shake free of the ropes. But her outbursts are fading, each shake slightly less violent than one before. Watching her eyes, I can see that she wants to strike out. An oil-stained cloth in her mouth gags her resistance, causing her to choke on her own fear and bile. A sheen of sweat polishes her tanned skin, adding a lustre to the flesh and a scent of spice which only makes my mistress hungrier. The sweat of human fear is tastier. Sweeter. Her skin is beginning to peel, burned by constant exposure to the sun before I found her. As my mistress feeds, I watch the terror in the woman's eyes and the silent, desperate plea for release from the tsunami of experience rushing through her body. From my vantage point beside a dust-covered bookshelf, I slowly shake my head. She is neither attractive nor remarkable. Deliberately so. We don't want to offer the ever watching media any special reason to be interested in this particular disappearance.

I've seen it so many times before that I walk outside and leave my mistress to her needs, grumbling a few words to myself just to hear my own voice. It is easy to forget how to speak, hiding here and there are still times when I need to communicate with others, to pretend to be normal. But I am, in essence, a baited lure dangling before the unsuspecting members of my own kind.

Spears of sunlight pierce the veil of trees. Rainbow dressed leaves flitter under twilight's steady glare. If you open your mouth, you can almost drink the moist air, feeling the dew condense on your tongue. Or cuddle it. The squeals and coughs of various animals sing a natural symphony to life. The golden casque of a cassowary disappears into the undergrowth.

Nestling between the rough, moss-haired bark of two ancient eucalypts, like a lover's head between legs of their desire, I can see where my hut sleeps securely. A faded CSIRO logo peels from the roughened wood of the walls, flakes of paint occasionally drifting to the ground like colored dandruff on the brown mud of the ground. Originally established as a place to watch the unfolding wonder of life, it now serves as a nest for our existence.

My heart starts beating a little faster, dancing to the now rhythmic beat of the woman's screams. My mistress will have removed the cloth for the final kill. She likes to hear the terror, to feel the vibrations of their curses as she drains the last of their resistance. Leaving just another foolish visitor lost in the tricky embrace of the Daintree. Normally my mistress would control herself and the bewildered tourist would wander from the warm moisture of the forest after a week or so into the blaze of snapping camera flashes and a huddle of television cameras. The wounds on their flesh would be attributed to the teeth of myriad of wildlife and the gentle needles of plants that attacked them as they wandered, dehydrated, through the forest. Any blood on their clothes is simply a badge of their survival, and the memories which haunt their dreams, the nightmares they can never share, are ignored as the result of starvation and fear.

But this time my mistress is hungry and the urge to procreate overwhelming.

Mounds of wounded flesh rose on my arms and neck, reminders of the times when there was no one else to satisfy my mistress's desires. I say mistress but you may as well call her my wife so often does my blood sustain her. We are bound. I love her. We had never shared the words or conducted any kind of ceremony. Such things are not part of her nature. We just are. Together. I love every delicious bite, every drop of my blood that dribbles over the ravines of her teeth. Decades ago I had entered the forest's embrace, unaware of the true mysteries held in its mossy fingers. As a young entomologist hoping to specialise in hemipterology, the warm colors of the Daintree seemed to me to be a kaleidoscope of invertebrates. Crustaceans, worms, beetles, ants, spiders, mites, scorpions, amblypygids, centipedes and millipedes, not to mention the snails and slugs, burrowed their way into the complex ecosystem that had survived virtually untouched by the machinations of man. Siren-like cicadas singing my dreams of a PhD into reality.

The screaming from my hut stops, replaced by the normal whispers and murmurs of the forest. I close my eyes, breathing these last few moments of rest. The nearest colony of crocodiles is at least a two day journey from the hut. The slowly stuttering waters crayoned brown with mud from the recent rains. I will head out as soon as my mistress leaves. The further away from the hut that body is found, the better. Hopefully it will never be found at all.

Every so often people from the CSIRO would come and visit the hut, camping inside while they conducted whatever research they were doing. We always moved out, hiding in the gentle care of the rainforest, and let them go. That was the deal I had made with my mistress so long ago. One of the few conditions of our relationship. While the deaths of a few foolish tourists could be hidden by the sapphire-misted mountains and the ring-barked forest, all tragic to the moon, the loss of a scientist would be harder to hide.

After my wife found me, I was forced to briefly return to the world thirty odd years ago to remove myself from its bland stagnancy . Forced to cut myself from the bureaucracy of everyday life before I could join her in the humid forest. I had come here, young, eager to make a name for myself, hoping to use the ancient footprints of the evolutionary past to draw a map for the future of humanity. I was looking for a blueprint written in insects. Increased knowledge. A desire to improve my mind. Instead I found something older than I ever dreamed, with a history that swallowed my science like a jacaranda drinks the mist.

Her.

She had lived in the forest for millions of years, oblivious to the rise of social media and civilisation. Empires grew and fell, brushing the silken hairlike strands of her awareness. No Christian crosses or Stars of David worried her or her kin; they didn't know what they were so they had no reason to fear. Only the harsh burning sun causes them to hide, safe under covered embrace of the forest's trees. I know I am little more than a convenience for them, the latest in a long line of handy servants. I don't care.

An explosion of sound, the squawking cries of startled galahs, the nervous hiccoughing of tiny tree frogs, vibrates through the forest as my mistress leaves. Moss covered tree trunks bend to escape her passage. A wombat grunts and buries itself in a mound of fallen leaves and bushes shuffle as the wallaroos scamper for another place to play. With a deep sigh, knowing that only a drained body awaits me inside the hut, I grab my old, torn body bag and go to collect the corpse.

I hear the whispers as I walk through the dirt-dressed street of what pretended to be an outback way station. From the skies above, it looks like a hole in a blanket of green. While the forest provides most things, it is painfully short of coffee trees and chocolate bushes. People stare at me. The crevassed bushie with the faded blue singlet and the rock scratched boots. Years of walking through the rainforest unprotected by suntan cream has stained my skin deep brown and I scraped some patches of mud from my knee-length shorts as I approached the tin-roofed buildings.

Mick's says the sign. No one needs to explain what Mick's is. Mick's is everything. Post Office. Bank. A clearing house for communicating with the rest of so-called civilization. Somewhere off the Upper Daintree Road, east of Bloomfield and south of Degerra, the place had a pub, Mick's, and no name.

'Hey, mate,' drawls a voice from behind the counter. Mick doesn't even look up from the pages of a two month old People magazine. I raise a hand, my open palm acknowledging his greeting. On a wall, hiding behind the Tim Tam laden shelves, there is a row of doors, gateways to boxes behind them. On one of them are the letters RMR. My initials.

'There's a box for you out the back,' Mick calls out. 'And I've packed up your usual stuff if you want to bring your ute round.'

I distractedly grunt a thank-you. Not that Mick cares. He returns to his magazine, reading an article about the NRL with the headline 'Who needs a Big Willie when you've got a great Tongue' referring to the latest round of player trading.

There's a letter in my mail box. Addressed to her. She doesn't get mail. As far as I know, she cannot even read. She certainly doesn't speak. I just know what she wants, as if the ideas arrive in my mind, skipping the artifice of language and plugging directly into my brain. My fingers run across the edges of the envelope, twisting down to trace the v-shaped smile of the lip at the back. There's no return address. No identifying information. There doesn't need to be.

Mick looks up again. 'Anything interesting,' he calls out, displaying a negligent curiosity. 'I didn't know if was a wrong address or what but I stuck it in the box for you anyway.'

'Not really. It's for someone I used to know.'

'Need me to send it back.'

I wave the envelope at him, indicating the lack of details. 'No need. I'll look after it.'

He shrugs, disrupting the dandruff that lines the shoulders of his faded flannel shirt. Finger-painted dust Mandelbrots stain clichéd art across the exposed singlet. Mick looks exactly how people expect him to look. At home, I'm sure he dresses in jeans and a t-shirt. And drinks shiraz instead of Fourex, for all I know.

I pick up some other supplies from the shelves, things I had once thought that I would never need again. Walking to the counter, I hand over my possessions including one of deodorant dispensers that spray a mist of scented beauty into the air.

'Planning a party?' Mick asks as an electronic beep records the prices. 'I thought you didn't care about this stuff?'

'I'll need some extra cans of gasoline as well.'

Mick's eyes narrow as he hands my credit card back. 'What's going on, mate? This ain't like you. Is it something to do with that letter?'

Lifting a 5 litre cask of insect repellent onto the floor, I look around the shop. I wonder if he knows that this will be my last visit. 'Yeah. I know who it is from and what they want.'

Dusk's gentle light cries farewell to the heat of the day as I enter the research hut. Placing my purchases on the table I stand still and breathe. No-one is there. Not even in my mind. I throw the letter on a wooden table leaning heavily against the wall. The envelope catches on the splintered surface, little claw-like tears scratching its surface. There is another envelope, just like it but thirty years older, lying abandoned in a drawer of my desk.

I wrote that one. I unpack my provisions, stacking them neatly in the limited cupboard space or under my camp-bed. I should turn the generator on to ensure the batteries are charged properly. The patterned sunlight through forest's hood holds things steady while I'm away but it isn't enough to fully recharge the deck of batteries that power the hut.

Tomorrow. I'll do it tomorrow.

I should also clean the various insect droppings, loose leaves and sheets of dust and life. More jobs for tomorrow.

Or for my replacement. That is what the letter represents. I know why. I have aged, my blood no longer boasts the rich sweetness of youth nor the refined maturity of middle age. I turn 60 next year and my blood is going stale. My mistress needs new flesh. The latest tourist probably convinced her of that. Or convinced her kin.

I close my eyes and she is there. A black mist shaped into the form of a woman. A charcoal drawing, made with a twig from a camp fire. Imprecise and imperfect, I can see the little jutting mounds on her skin as she keeps this form.

My heart skips an erratic thump as I fall in love again.

'You know,' she says. The words form in my head, not in English, so clear that it is a language that transcends all languages.

'Yes,' I reply, still using my voice even though it is not necessary. She smiles, amused by my small rebellion.

'The other slaves give up the need to open their mouths.'

'I need the practice for when I collect the supplies from town.'

She nods, a ripple of anticipation canyoning down her black flesh. Unlike those before me, I knew other loves. Other obsessions. I came here, long ago, looking for bugs to teach me about the ways of life and the intricacies of nature. I found more than I ever imagined. These creatures were beautiful. Deadly but beautiful. How could explain that I wanted to live? I am just livestock to them. Two legged cattle roaming the land until the time comes from me to become the latest BBQ.

My wife could never understand my reluctance to die. That was the way the forest worked. Co-dependence. There is no malice in her decision. I can no longer fulfill the duties for which I was kept. In the same way people in the city take an arthritic pet to the vet or a farmer kills a pig to feed their family, my fate has been sealed from the moment I accepted her offer to become her slave. The law of the forest.

And I understand the necessity of what must happen next. The very concept of divorce is foreign to her. I am useless, therefore I am finished.

My wife glides around the hut, a creaking grunt echoing as she shuts the windows. The door seals with a click. There is no escape. We are trapped here, together, as it must be.

My wife and her family can never be revealed to the masses of humanity. They would be killed. Just like my wonderful insects. Scientists still don't know how the evolution of insects relates the to the evolution of other animal groups. They are the loners of the animal kingdom, the children who only play with their own kind. Their ties are closer with plants. Yet we think of them as pests, we try to kill them with chemicals and genetically manipulated bioagents. On the whole, humanity fails to learn from insects. Fails to appreciate the awe of something different.

I sit on the camp bed in the corner and briefly close my eyes. 'I am ready.'

'You have served well.'

'Thank you.'

I turn my head to look at her. My mistress, my wife, begins to break down, her body shattering into hundreds of tiny mosquitoes, a previously unidentified Culex subgenus. The reverberating buzz fills the room. She doesn't like sunlight, preferring the cooler hues of dawn and dusk. It doesn't matter. There will be no more days for either of us. Original bloodsuckers, more than 150 million years old, they evolved in ways no-one had conceived. In meeting her, I absorbed more, learnt more, than I ever dreamt. Through her, I became better. She is my evolution.

The first mosquitoes bite into my skin, the poison coating my flesh killing them instantly. With a violent screech that threatens to shake my mind into a billion pieces, my wife swarms.

Slowly, deliberately, I press the nozzle to release the chemicals from the pesticide into the air with a drawn-out hiss, the invisible gas filling the sealed space. It is based on Allium sativum L., minced dehydrated garlic.

I smile. There is no escape. For either of us.

Hundreds of tiny bites pierce my skin, no longer feeding, just seeking raw revenge. Wave after wave fall to the ground. My wife cannot reform her human shape and open the windows to free herself.

I cannot breathe without swallowing some of her. We merge in a way we have never done before.

My eyes close, huge welts from the multitude of bites pressing them shut. This is death. The bounce of my heart is slowing, the air in my lungs turning stale and frustrated by its inability to escape.

Unable to talk, I whisper my final words in my mind, knowing she will hear, hoping she will understand.

'I love you. Until death do us part.'

**Renfield's Wife** originally appeared in the 2011 anthology *Dead Red Heart*, edited by Russell B. Farr

**Damon Cavalchini** doesn't exist. He was allegedly a member of the Management Committee of the Aurealis Awards, Australia's premier speculative fiction literary awards, for more than six years and served a three year term as the President of Fantastic Queensland, an organization dedicated to providing opportunities for Australian spec-fic writers as punishment for his ongoing crimes against literature.

Apart from his biography, his fiction has been mainly confined to acquittal reports and business documents. His short story, "Renfield's Wife", was published in the 2011 anthology, *Dead Red Heart*, and made Ellen Datlow's Honourable Mention list for the year's best horror. Other tales include the "Tenth Life of Sargeant Tom" in *Journeys of the Mind* — an Anthology of Speculative Fiction, "The Twenty-Fifth Day" in *Ain't No Sanity Clause*, "Furst Noel" in *Sanity Clause is Coming*, "The Second Death of Manya Akinova" and "Fairy Nights" (both in *Starburst*), "If I Could But Shiver" in *Grimmer and Grimmer 3* and "Electric You" and "Shelved Desires" (both in *Andromeda's Children*).

He's also written and directed for local theatre but nobody went to see it. Should you still be reading, please wait for the people in white jackets to arrive.

# LAST RITES

# Rough Trade
## By Elizabeth R. McClellan

I found the secret to life, revealed
by my master and the sciences: blood,
carrying vitality from fly to moth to bird
to cat, damnably quick as they are.

Insurance ran out, phone cut off, waiting
for him to call me through the aether, appear
in the mist beside the river where I sleep.
During the day I have the library, to study

the alignment of the veins, to post ads,
discreet, for those who like the needle and blade.
The nice doctor got me on PreP, though it
won't matter when I ascend to sit by

his left hand, the place of the faithful
servant. But it is new and we don't know
if he could sicken, so I take my meds,
make friends at the clinic with twinks bearing

telltale scars. They are ecstasy, for a time.
They do not scratch. My greedy lapping
turns some of them on. They slip me cash,
drugs I'll trade later, since I must not offer

him less than purest vintage. He says pot
tastes of mold, speed like electric bananas
and hot metal, the antipsychotics I stopped
like wet flour and electricity. I long to develop

my palate: I only taste copper, smell
adrenaline sweat. I am very good at stitching
my boys back together when I am overeager,
though I try to maintain control.

I do not want to be like the writhing wives
lost to bloodlust and desire, no thoughts
but eating and exulting. The love between men,
said the ancient philosophers, is best in life,

though I wonder what they disguised under
effusive praise of reason and equals.
Mina is no mindless bride, after all, and I know
she holds his heart in thrall as he holds me,

without a drop of red passed between them.
Eternity is long and the master's house
has rooms and table settings sufficient for
three times as many. I wish he would call

for me. I feel him too far, and I ache.
I tell the rats earnestly all the news, to bear back
to where he scurries unseen at his leisure.
They know I never harm them, remove the cats

that wander too near the water; they are thankful,
as me to him, the promise of more life powerful
even lacking eternity. They nestle with me
when the wind blows cold, blanket me

warm as a well-loved infant, their tails squirming
kisses on my skin. I free their kings
with clever fingers. Word spreads until
I have a den of servants, furry facsimiles

of my thralls to come, who bring me food
but not my friend, who has surely not forgotten
his most faithful acolyte. I bring a boy,
barely a man and blue with cold, to my burrow.

When he is done screaming he sees how
they do not bite or scratch, joins me under
the living duvet, lets me bite his tongue
until his life flows down my throat and

his cries are begging for more in joy,
writhing against me in the warm dark as I
drink all of him, content to wait here
for my ascension, for his coming.

**Elizabeth R. McClellan** is a white disabled neurospicy sapphic gender/queer demisexual poet writing on unceded Quapaw and Chickasha Yaki land. Ka is a domestic violence attorney working with refugee and immigrant survivors. Kans work has appeared in Nightmare Magazine, The Future Fire and many others including the MOTHER: TALES OF LOVE AND TERROR anthology from Weird Little Worlds Press. Find kan online as popelizbet or at functionalmuse.club.